"I can't, It's not right. You don't trust me."

It was on the tip of his tongue to deny it, to tell her his trust in her grew the more time he spent with her. He stopped himself when he realized how it would sound if he uttered those words.

She'd think he was saying it just to get her into bed.

He cursed under his breath and sat up. It felt like ripping off his own skin to separate himself from her warm, soft, supple body. He clamped his eyes shut and raked his fingers through his hair.

"You don't trust me, either," he muttered.

He glanced back at her, sorely tempted to touch her again…to draw her close. Her eyes looked huge in her delicate face. She wrapped her arms beneath her breasts, hugging herself. He was reminded of her vulnerability.

"Will you let me spend time with you now?" he asked. "For more than just tonight?"

Dear Reader,

I've often reflected upon how one action in time can have a ripple effect, how one choice can end up having huge consequences for generations to come. Deidre Kavanaugh, the heroine of *One in a Billion,* is at the mercy of choices that her mother made even before she was born. She's the "secret baby" all grown up. She discovers her biological father, only to lose him, and in a matter of months, her life is forever altered when she falls hard for the wrong man—her biological father's surrogate son and the coheir to his company and vast fortune. Nick Malone reigns in a world where rational decision making rules, but beautiful, feisty, independent Deidre has the tendency to drive logic straight out of his brain.

It's not easy to forgive when wounds run so deep, to trust when one has known betrayal, to see faults in another, and yet still love. This is Deidre's challenge, and her story is the perfect culmination of the Kavanaugh family's struggles and triumphs. I hope you enjoy this love story about two very unique and memorable individuals and the power of forgiveness and acceptance.

Beth Kery

ONE IN A BILLION

BY
BETH KERY

MILLS & BOON

First published in Great Britain 2012
by Mills & Boon, an imprint of Harlequin (UK) Limited,
Eton House, 18-24 Paradise Road, Richmond, Surrey TW9 1SR

© Beth Kery 2012

ISBN: 978 0 263 89474 5
ebook ISBN: 978 1 408 97863 4

23-1012

Harlequin (UK) policy is to use papers that are natural, renewable and recyclable products and made from wood grown in sustainable forests. The logging and manufacturing processes conform to the legal environmental regulations of the country of origin.

Printed and bound in Spain
by Blackprint CPI, Barcelona

Beth Kery holds a doctorate in the behavioral sciences and enjoys incorporating what she's learned about human nature into her stories. To date, she has published more than a dozen novels and short stories, and she writes in multiple genres, always with the overarching theme of passionate, emotional romance. To find out about the Harbor Town series, visit Beth at her website, www.BethKery.com, or join her for a chat at her reader group, www.groups.yahoo.com/group/BethKery.

This story brings me full circle
in the Home to Harbor Town series,
so I'd like to thank all the readers who have
supported the books thus far in addition to everyone
who contributed to its evolution: my agent, Laura
Bradford, my editor, Susan Litman, beta readers Lea,
Mary and Sandy and of course, my husband,
who is forever patient with my never-ending questions
about business transactions or the specifics
of how this or that piece of machinery actually works.
My deepest appreciation to you all.

Chapter One

Clutching one of the delicate centerpieces from her brother's wedding reception, Deidre Kavanaugh walked out of the near-empty ballroom alone. She was beyond grateful to have witnessed Liam's happiness at marrying the love of his life—Natalie Reyes—tonight. Now that family and friends were gone, however, and the romance and gaiety of the wedding was over, she couldn't help but feel a little disappointed to be flying solo.

Again.

She didn't have to be alone, of course. Staying at Cedar Cottage instead of at her sister Colleen's had been Deidre's choice. She was used to her solitary ways at this point in her life, and old habits died hard.

Of course, her mother, Brigit, had invited Deidre to stay at the family home on Sycamore Avenue. Deidre had politely refused and then tried to harden her heart when she saw her mother's hurt, sad expression. Her refusal couldn't have been too surprising, considering that Deidre held such anger toward her mother for keeping the identity of her biological father a secret for so many years. Deidre had only learned Lincoln DuBois was her natural father late last summer. If it hadn't been for Liam and his Natalie's investigation into their past, Brigit would have taken the secret to the grave with her.

A million stars sparkled against the backdrop of an ebony night sky when she walked out of the Starling Hotel. Liam and Natalie had chosen a windless, frigid night to celebrate their marriage. She took a deep breath when she walked out onto the steps, but it didn't help much to revive her. The last three months of her life had been stressful…life-altering. She'd learned the identity of her biological father and then lost him to cancer within months of gaining that knowledge.

Deidre was exhausted, body and soul.

She paused on the steps, inspecting the little town by starlight. It seemed surreal to be back in Harbor Town. The quaint little community had once been the site of so much childhood innocence and bliss. It'd also been the place where she'd made the horrific discovery she wasn't really Derry Kavanaugh's daughter. Derry had had that truth confirmed on the same night. His consequent ragged emotional state was what had led to a traumatic car crash in which Derry had been killed along with three others. Deidre had left Harbor Town the summer before college and never returned—until last night.

She was in the process of searching for her rental car keys in her evening bag, clutching at the floral centerpiece the whole time, when a man called out to her. She came to an abrupt halt in the parking lot, her breath sticking in her lungs. She recognized that clipped, authoritative voice.

Nick Malone. Hearing it so unexpectedly here in Harbor Town set her immediately on edge. For some reason, one of the first things Nick had ever said to her when she told him about her discovery that she was Lincoln DuBois's biological daughter popped into her brain at that moment.

You must have thought you woke up one day and won the lottery.

She spun around. His shadow looked large and imposing against the backdrop of the night sky.

"What are you doing here?" she asked Nick breathlessly.

"We have important things to discuss. I would think that's obvious, following Lincoln's death."

His face was difficult to make out in the dim light, but what Deidre couldn't see, she filled in from memory—the rugged, bold features, the cool, suspicious gaze that always seemed to be detailing her flaws.

"I can't believe you came here."

"I can't believe you thought for a second I wouldn't find you, wherever you went," he replied dryly. "You knew the reading of Lincoln's will took place yesterday at The Pines," he continued, referring to Lincoln's palatial lodge on the edge of Lake Tahoe.

Deidre shifted in her high heels anxiously. "My brother's wedding was tonight. But you must already know or you wouldn't have shown up here. I guess you've been giving more work to that private investigator you hired to snoop into my personal life."

Her gaze dropped to his coat-draped, broad shoulders when he shrugged. "Nothing so melodramatic. Your sister Colleen told me about the wedding after Linc's funeral. It didn't take a detective to figure out you were probably here. As to your personal life, that pretty much became my business the day you told me about your claim to be Lincoln DuBois's daughter."

She tamped down her flare of temper at his arrogant presumption. "Lincoln was my father. I just wanted to *know* him. I've told you from day one I don't care about Lincoln's money or your precious company," she said, referring to her biological father's multibillion-dollar conglomerate, DuBois Enterprises, where Nick acted as chief executive officer. Nick not only ran Lincoln's company: he was Lincoln's protégé and like a surrogate son to her newfound father. As such, he seemed to think it was his business to question her every move and treat her like a conniving gold digger. It seemed an utter impossibility to convince him that she had no designs whatsoever on Lincoln's wealth. She gave an exasperated sigh when he stubbornly remained silent. "Why should you care where I go? What difference does it make what I do, now that Lincoln has passed away?"

"It makes a difference. Look, why don't we go and find a place to have a cup of coffee and talk?"

"There's really nothing left for us to talk about. Besides, didn't you interrogate me enough at The Pines?" she said. Deidre had lived there, nursing her newly found father until he'd finally succumbed to a brain tumor last week.

"Interrogate? You hardly ever stuck around long enough for me to ask *a* question, let alone *interrogate* you. You avoided me like the plague whenever we were both at The Pines. If you would just consider the matter rationally for a moment, you'd see the importance of me understanding your motives…of knowing you better. Lincoln entrusted me with his company. It's my job to protect his interests."

Deidre glanced away guiltily. She *had* avoided Nick a lot, but she told herself she'd done so because she didn't care for Nick's patronizing manner. In truth, her avoidance *might* have had something to do with her reaction to him as a man. Nick Malone was the last man on the planet she should find attractive.

She shivered, whether it was from anger or anxiety over Nick's unexpected presence, she couldn't say. "I'm *not* interested in Lincoln's estate or DuBois Enterprises. I wanted to know him as best I could, given the short time we had. Why is that so hard for you to comprehend?"

His head went back, his indrawn breath hissing against his teeth. She sensed his profound frustration, but given how bewildering his presence here was, she had a hard time feeling sorry for him. Wasn't her life complicated enough without Nick? She shivered again.

"It's freezing out here, and there's something important I need to tell you," he muttered. He reached out and cupped her elbow. "Will you at least sit in my car so I can turn on the heat?"

Those sharp eyes of his didn't miss much, she recalled. Something in his tense, strained manner sent a distant alarm going off in her head.

"Is it really that important?"

"More important than you know."

"All right," she said cautiously after a moment. She took a step, breaking their contact. His touch unsettled her. He waved to the left and tilted his head.

She followed him into the next row of cars. He hit the remote lock with his thumb and a dark sedan's headlights blinked. Deidre sat when he opened the door for her, placing the floral arrangement on the floor next to her feet. She said nothing when he got in the car and turned on the ignition, but she was highly aware of him. The dim dash lights made it possible for her to make a covert study of him. Nick was the type of man who dominated a room once he entered it. Inside a car, his presence crowded rational thought completely out of her mind.

He wore a suit and an attractive black cashmere dress coat, making her wonder if he'd been prepared to enter Liam's wedding reception to find her. Deidre had immediately understood upon being introduced to Nick that while he may possess a handsome face and the fit, lean body of an athlete and horseman, he wasn't about looks.

He was about power.

The walking embodiment of an alpha-male tycoon, Nick conquered the business world just like cowboys had vanquished the intimidating, rugged landscapes of the American West.

She wouldn't let him conquer her with the same heavy-handed tactics.

He gripped the steering wheel with gloved hands. She tensed, waiting for his attack.

"You're pale," he muttered. "Have you been sick?"

Deidre's jaw dropped open. She looked at him in amazement, but he kept his face turned in profile. His gruff solicitation was the last thing she'd expected.

"You can tell I'm pale by examining me in a dark parking lot?" she asked, saying the first thing that came to mind to cover her embarrassment.

"I saw you at the reception, dancing with that man."

"You actually came into the ballroom?"

"I just stood in the door, looking for you." He ignored Deidre's exasperated sigh. "Who was he?"

She did a double take. "Who was *who*?"

"The man you were dancing with."

Deidre blinked. She'd forgotten Nick wasn't at The Pines last autumn when her brother Marc had visited to offer her support.

"It was my brother Marc. Can you please get on with whatever is so important?"

"You can't just run away from all this, Deidre. It's naive of you, or stubborn, or both to think you can say you're Lincoln DuBois's daughter and not expect any ramifications to that claim. Why won't you agree to the genetic testing, at the very least?"

Nervousness fluttered in her stomach. She'd been expecting him to broach this topic. Just the term *genetic testing* had taken on an electrical charge in the past few months. Unbeknownst to Nick, she'd already had the testing done. She'd refused to comply when Nick and DuBois Enterprises's chief legal officer, John Kellerman, insisted upon it. Mostly she'd ignored their demands because they'd made them in such a condescending, suspicious manner. Her body wasn't the property of DuBois Enterprises, and as far as she was concerned, its representatives had no right to make demands upon it. When Lincoln had requested the same thing, however, she'd immediately agreed.

But he'd died before they'd received the results.

What if she *wasn't* Lincoln's daughter? Deidre wondered for the thousandth time. The thought caused a familiar raw ache to expand in her belly. It frightened her a little, to consider how much hope she'd invested in being Lincoln's natural child. If she wasn't Lincoln's, she'd be right back where she'd been for most of her entire adult life.

An outsider. Anchorless. Different. Fatherless.

"Deidre?" Nick prompted quietly. She blinked. Had he noticed her anxiety? She took a deep breath.

"I've already had the genetic testing done at a place called GenLabs in Carson City."

"You did?" he asked intently.

She nodded.

"When?"

"About three weeks ago. Lincoln asked me to have it done, but he died before we got the results," she said, her hushed voice quaking. From the periphery of her vision she saw his hand came off his thigh jerkily, but then he replaced it. A strained silence followed. For a split second, she'd thought he meant to touch her...to comfort, before logic had set in.

Her heart thrummed louder in her ears as she stared fixedly out the front window.

"And?" he asked in a subdued tone.

"They told me at the lab that the results would take up to seven weeks. We should have the results before Christmas. They agreed to call me and tell me the final result before they send out the report."

She turned when he exhaled raggedly. He looked tense.

"What's wrong? Aren't you glad that I've had the testing? It's what you and John Kellerman and everybody at DuBois wanted all along."

"Of course I'm glad. Now there's nothing to do but get to know one another better. And wait."

"Why should the results matter so much to you? I won't make any claims on Lincoln's assets one way or another."

He laughed softly...mirthlessly. He had dimples. It had struck her as amazing the first time she'd met him to see those two indentations in such a formidable face. She recalled how once she'd seen some graffiti painted on a craggy rock face of the mountains several miles outside of the Bagram Air Base in Afghanistan—a smiley face grinning innocuously from a war zone.

She had a similar reaction to Nick's dimples.

"You make it sound so simple," he murmured.

"It *is* simple."

"It *never* was simple, and it just got exponentially more complicated."

"What are you talking about?" she asked slowly.

"I came to Harbor Town to tell you that Lincoln had a new will drawn up. He's left you half of the wealth and property he didn't leave to charity. He's also left you a fifty percent controlling interest in DuBois Enterprises."

"What?" she asked numbly.

"You're an heiress, Deidre. The way things stand right now, you're one of the wealthiest women in the country."

She might have heard the flutter of a butterfly's wings in the ensuing silence. She inhaled slowly, trying to ground herself. This could *not* be happening.

And yet...what was that strange, warm, wonderful feeling growing deep down in her belly?

He made me his heiress. Lincoln truly *did believe I was his daughter. His faith was his proof. Lincoln hadn't required the scientific variety.*

Something shivered through her. It took Deidre a moment to recognize the feeling as pure joy.

Nick decided that if Deidre Kavanaugh had had any part in manipulating Linc to alter his will in her favor, she certainly was one hell of an actress. Every nuance of her face and body suggested she was utterly stunned by the news she was an heiress to a massive fortune.

"He didn't," she whispered, obviously in shock.

"He did."

"Lincoln can't have meant it. There must be a mistake. I'm a nurse, not a businesswoman," she said hollowly.

"From your reaction, am I to assume you didn't have prior knowledge of the change of will?"

"I had no idea," she said. Her spine stiffened when he cocked one eyebrow in a show of subtle disbelief, testing her. She leaned across the console toward him. He caught the subtle scent of her floral perfume and, for a few seconds, his thoughts scattered. Deidre had a way of making him forget practical goals and objectives.

"I resent your tone," she said. "I suppose you have it all worked out, don't you? You figure I manipulated and cajoled a sick, vulnerable man into leaving me all his money, is that it?"

"What have I told you, time and again while we were at The Pines together, Deidre?" he murmured softly.

She snapped her jaw closed. He found himself studying her beautiful face cast in the dim dashboard lights. What *was* it her? Her elegance mingled with a sort of bad-girl charm. She fascinated him, whether he wanted to be fascinated or not.

"That you're Lincoln's man," she answered his question, her chin tilted at the stubborn angle to which he'd grown all too accustomed. "That you'll do whatever is in your power to make sure his wishes are carried out," she quoted the familiar refrain.

He nodded. Their meetings at The Pines had been few and fleeting, not to mention charged. Nevertheless, Nick was glad to hear he'd imparted that particular message loud and clear to her.

"There's something else I want you to know," Nick said.

"What?"

"Until I can rest assured you're his daughter, that Lincoln was of sound mind when he drew up the new will, and that you had no part in coercing Lincoln's actions in the last days of his life, I plan to contest the will."

She flinched as if he'd just slapped her. Regret spiked through his awareness, the strength of it catching him off guard. She'd gotten under his skin. He could understand why Lincoln had been so taken by her. But the fact remained, the way things stood, there was a good chance Deidre and he would be sitting across a courtroom from each other sometime in the near future. He had no right to find her fascinating.

"You just don't get it," she said, her low voice shaking with fury. "I nursed and cared for Lincoln with every ounce of compassion and skill I possess. Ask any of the servants, or the hospice nurses, or Dr. Leland. Everything I did, I did with the hope of having him for another day…another minute."

"That may be true. I'm suspending judgment on the matter."

She gave an incredulous bark of laughter. "Suspending judgment until when?"

"Until I have the opportunity to observe you, understand your character, your motivations, your life. I'll be staying in Harbor Town for the next few days or weeks or however long it takes to do that."

"Who says *I* plan to stay in Harbor Town?"

He shrugged. "I'll make a point to go wherever you go. I hope you'll cooperate with this. If you've got nothing to hide, why should it matter if I spend time with you and get to know you better?"

"Why don't you just get that private investigator you hired before to do it?" she asked scathingly.

"I don't trust his powers of observation as much as I do my own." He held her stare. He watched as her expression went slack in disbelief as she realized he was dead serious.

"You're crazy," she whispered.

"No," he corrected. "I'm determined. And I'm committed to the health and well-being of DuBois Enterprises and its thousands of employees."

She made a sound of disgust, but Nick was undaunted. He studied her in the dim light. She'd combed her short, golden blond hair behind her ears, where it curled in gleaming waves. It looked silken soft. She was clearly a beauty, but it wasn't her physical attributes that made him want to touch her—at least not entirely. It was the way Deidre carried herself, the way she moved with a careless grace and bone-deep confidence. Without ever trying, she was a classic American beauty with an edge. A perfect, prickly, long-stemmed rose…

…Grace Kelly with a serious attitude.

Beautiful, fierce and fascinating Deidre may be, but he'd come here with a mission. Either he'd determine that Deidre was somehow unworthy of Linc's estate or he'd gain her compliance. It just wasn't an option to be left at the helm of DuBois Enterprises without any real control, watching helplessly while the great company crashed, taking thousands of employees and dependents down with it.

"What are you really doing here, Nick?" she asked warily.

"I've told you. I'm here to learn more about you. If I'm given the opportunity to get to know you for a period of time without you avoiding me, I'll come to a conclusion about you. We can move on regarding Lincoln's last will and testament."

"So what…you plan to *investigate* me? Stalk me? Harass my friends and family? Lurk around and take pictures of me through a telephoto lens?"

"Would I catch anything interesting?" he asked, hiding a smile.

"I'd make sure you did," she promised so menacingly he raised his eyebrows. Seeing her slender, elegant figure swathed in a sophisticated dress had temporarily made him forget Deidre was a warrior. The background report he'd commissioned had painted a picture of a courageous, headstrong, fiercely independent woman who refused to settle down into any traditional path. She was not only a collegiate championship diver; she'd been an expert trick skier, financing much of her college education by performing in water shows. Her military record was stellar. She'd even been awarded a medal for entering an active area of combat to save one of her patients when a field hospital had been unexpectedly attacked.

"You can't plan on staying in Harbor Town," she continued, looking at him like he was possibly mad. "It's hardly a place for movers and shakers."

"I'll manage. I work on the road all the time. The hotel is offering me decent business facilities. I've made it clear at company headquarters that we'll keep my presence here under wraps for a while. I don't want the press getting hold of the story about the will yet. It's going to become a media frenzy when they do find out."

"*This* hotel?" Deidre asked, pointing at the building behind them.

He nodded.

She closed her eyes and he sensed it again, her extreme fatigue, her vulnerability.

"There's another reason we should spend some time getting to know each other better, Deidre."

She opened her eyes. He couldn't see their hue in the dim light emanating from the dashboard, but he knew they were an unusual blue-gray color. He could clearly see the line of her jaw and the delicate shell shape of her ear.

Was she made so perfectly everywhere?

"I'm afraid to ask," she murmured.

"Lincoln wrote me a letter before he died. He specifically asked me to get to know you better."

"Why?" she demanded. She leaned toward him, her fatigue seemingly disappearing at the mention of the man she believed to be her father. Her curiosity bordered on hunger. It struck him as understandable, but sad, that she was so desperate for information about Linc. Again, he inhaled her clean, floral feminine scent. His muscles clenched tight in restraint.

"Linc knew I had my doubts about your claim to be his child. Maybe he thought us spending time together would put those doubts to rest. He likely also knew that no one else could teach you about your inheritance as well as I could."

"Can I read the letter?"

"No."

She started at his abruptness.

He shut his eyes briefly when he saw her hurt, incredulous expression. Lincoln's letter had been heartbreakingly honest, almost childlike in its plea. Nick had been moved deeply by that letter, but at the same time, it'd made him question whether or not Lincoln was of sound mind when he'd changed his will. He couldn't tell Deidre that, though. She'd just accuse him of causing his prejudice against her to influence his opinion about Lincoln's motivations and state of mind.

"Not now you can't, Deidre," he said quietly. "I have my reasons for saying that. Don't take offense. Please."

But she had taken offense, he realized. Her backbone went ramrod straight.

"May I ask why it is that you believe you have the right to constantly call my morals and character into question, why you have the right to *investigate* me like a common criminal, when I don't even have the right to ask a simple thing of you?"

"I didn't mean you can't ask me things," he grated out.

"It sounded that way to me," she said, picking up her evening bag from her lap and retrieving the centerpiece from the floorboard. She reached for the car door and then suddenly went still, her hand outstretched. She turned, her brow crinkled in consternation. Her mouth fell open as if something had just dawned on her.

"Wait a second…" she muttered.

"What?"

"The other half of Lincoln's estate—he left it to *you*, didn't he?"

"Yes," Nick admitted.

The weighty silence was shattered by Deidre's desperate bark of laughter.

"Do you mean to tell me—"

"That's right," he said more calmly than he felt. "My hands are tied without you. There's a major acquisition deal

I've been brokering now for months, for instance, and even though the time is ripe for DuBois Enterprises to buy, I'm powerless to act without your consent. The way things stand legally right now, I can't make a major decision on behalf of DuBois Enterprises without your agreement. So for the time being, we're partners. Whether we like it or not."

Chapter Two

The next morning Deidre called Colleen, in much need of some sisterly commiseration and support. They met up at Jake's Place, a popular Harbor Town hangout, for brunch. Colleen's fork halted in midair when Deidre told her all the bizarre, gory details from her meeting with Nick the previous night.

"Lincoln left you half of his estate and fifty percent controlling interest in his company?" Colleen asked, clearly flabbergasted.

Deidre nodded and sipped her coffee.

"But he was one of the wealthiest men in the country. That means…you're bloody rich, Deidre."

Deidre chuckled at her sister's bald statement. "Not if Nick Malone has his say in the matter. He told me he plans to contest the will if he decides I coerced Lincoln in any way."

"*Coerced*," Colleen said, looking insulted. "You mean he suspects you took advantage of Lincoln? What's he think?

That you drugged him and stuck a pen in his hand, telling him to sign a new will? That's the most ridiculous thing I've ever heard. You're a skilled nurse and a compassionate woman. I've never seen someone so dedicated and concerned about another human being as you were that sweet, fragile man. Doesn't Nick even *know* you?"

Deidre smiled, heartened by her sister's show of faith in her. She would have been lost if it weren't for Colleen being at her side after Lincoln had died. She was the perfect confidant, since she'd witnessed firsthand Nick's suspicion of her.

"According to Nick, he *doesn't.* That's the whole problem," Deidre sighed, setting a forkful of pancakes down on her plate. It was hard to eat when her life felt like an out-of-control carnival ride.

"And Nick said he's here to investigate you?" Colleen asked as she resumed eating.

"Not exactly, no," Deidre admitted. "He said he needs an opportunity to observe me, determine my character. But it all amounts to the same thing, doesn't it? He's already convinced I'm a gold digger, so I'm sure he'll see whatever he expects to see."

She noticed Colleen's pensive expression as she ate her omelet. "*What?*"

"Why did Lincoln do it?" Colleen wondered. "Why would he split his estate and the control of his company equally between you and Nick?"

"I have no idea. Especially when I specifically told him I didn't want or expect anything from him. I have a hard enough time balancing my checkbook. How in the world could I possibly make decisions about a multibillion-dollar conglomerate?" Her gaze sharpened on her sister. "Do you think he did it because he wasn't in his right mind?" she asked in a hushed, worried tone. If that were the case, it was possible Lincoln's faith that she was his daughter was part of a demented delirium, as well.

"We both know Lincoln's level of consciousness fluctuated because of the tumor. He was sharp as a tack at times, but in others he was really out of it. It's my understanding that for the will to be binding, his attorney and other witnesses would have to attest he was in his right mind when he signed the document. But that's not what I was wondering about just now. You don't suppose there's any possibility that Lincoln arranged things this way so that you and Nick were *forced* to spend time with one another, do you?" Colleen asked tentatively.

"Why would he do that?"

Colleen's shrug was a little too nonchalant for Deidre's liking. "Maybe he noticed the sparks between you two and was doing a little matchmaking with his will."

Deidre rolled her eyes. "Those sparks are purely from dislike on my part and outright suspicion on Nick's. He suspects I manipulated a vulnerable, sick man into leaving me billions of dollars. How can you think he would be remotely interested in me in the romantic sense?" Deidre asked, her cheeks heating.

Was the fact that she found Nick attractive really so evident for everyone to see? Colleen's comment had called to mind Nick's reference to the letter Lincoln had left him. She hadn't told Colleen about that letter yet. For some reason, Lincoln making the request of Nick to get to know her better struck her as highly significant…highly intimate.

"So you're definitely not attracted to Nick Malone?" Colleen asked, her eyelids narrowed as she studied her.

"It's sort of hard to be attracted to someone when they're looking at you like you're a slimy criminal," she sidestepped.

"Yeah, I see what you mean. Well one thing is pretty straightforward. Nick Malone is gorgeous. He's at the top of every most eligible bachelor's list." She gave Deidre an *I'm just stating the truth* glance when Deidre looked at her incredulously. "You don't believe me? I looked Nick up online while we were staying at The Pines."

"*Colleen*," Deidre chastised, grinning. She'd frequently teased her sister while they were in Tahoe that she should surgically get her hand grafted to her iPad for convenience sake. Living in the Middle East and Europe for as long as she did, Deidre didn't share her fellow Americans' reliance on personal modern technology.

"Check this out," Colleen said, reaching inside her bag and withdrawing her iPad. A few seconds later she handed the tablet across the table. Deidre took it with a mixture of doubt, amusement and curiosity.

An image of Nick was on the screen. He was leading a sophisticated brunette with legs that went clear to her armpits out of the back of a black sedan. The woman wore an elaborate hat that probably had cost the equivalent of Deidre's annual salary as a nurse. Beneath the photo, Deidre read the inscription, *Churchill Downs—Nick Malone, chief executive officer of DuBois Enterprises, and Danielle Geddy, of the Geddy Banking Trust, attend the Derby Festival Preview Party.* The woman's smile was like headlight beams. Nick looked somber, as usual, and perhaps a tad irritated as he pinned the photographer with his icy stare.

"There's more," Colleen said wryly from across the table.

Deidre swiped her finger along the screen, her curiosity growing despite herself. Here was another photo, this one in profile, of Nick at a charity function, this time with an attractive blonde on his arm. Another showed him behind a podium wearing a suit and addressing a crowd. The caption said the occasion had been his acceptance of an honorary doctorate in business from a prestigious East Coast university. Nick didn't appear surly in this photo, as he had in the first. He did look somber, intent…and drop-dead gorgeous.

"He looks especially good in that one," Colleen observed, reading Deidre's mind.

Deidre laughed. "What's your point, Colleen?"

"I'm just saying that most of the world sees Nick Malone in a completely different light than you do."

"Given the strange circumstances, that's not too surprising, is it?"

"No, I understand that. I'm just pointing out that Nick is considered by most to be a brilliant businessman, not to mention a heck of a catch. *And*…"

"And *what?*" Deidre asked warily when she noticed her sister's significant glance.

"It occurred to me on one or a dozen occasions while we were at The Pines that there was an attraction between the two of you. I used to notice Nick watching you quite a bit, Dee," Colleen said, grinning. "You light a fire in him. He's got an itch for you."

"You're being ridiculous," Deidre exclaimed, stabbing her fork into her sausage patty with undue force.

"Am I?"

"If you've noticed any sparks of that variety coming from him, I'm willing to bet the reason isn't unquenchable lust."

"What do you mean?" Colleen wondered.

Deidre shrugged, not wanting to give the impression she actually had thought about the topic overly much. Even though she had.

"I think he's testing me by acting interested every once in a while. He already thinks I'm a conniving, immoral female. Maybe he thinks if he can seduce me, he'll get me to show my true colors. He'll prove to himself that I'm a gold digger by using himself as bait."

Colleen set her coffee mug down heavily on the table. "Do

you really think so? Nick has struck me as cool and unapproachable at times—intimidating, even—but do you really believe he could be that manipulative?"

"He certainly suspects I'm that manipulative, so I don't feel very guilty for thinking the same of him," Deidre said.

She turned pensive as she stared out the window on to Main Street, which had been festively decorated for the holidays. *Christmas in Harbor Town,* she thought with wistful sadness. How lovely it would be to be like Colleen, to feel that she truly belonged here…that she wasn't an outsider looking in. She'd belonged there once, as a child.

That was the past, though. She felt like even more of an imposter at the idea of being Lincoln's heiress in the present.

"I don't know what to think, Colleen," she admitted after a pause, meeting Colleen's gaze. "The only thing I know for certain is that Lincoln made me a player in a game with stakes so high, I can't even comprehend them. I'm a fish out of water. And truthfully? I don't know *what* a man like Nick would do to ensure he maintains control of a company that possesses the revenues of some small countries' entire economies. Do you?"

Colleen's face settled into a solemn expression, and Deidre had her answer.

Deidre promised her sister she'd rest and take it easy that afternoon. Colleen had been expressing concern for her lack of appetite and difficulty sleeping since Lincoln had died. Her life had been a blur since Lincoln's death last week and her hurried trip to Harbor Town for Liam's wedding.

She returned to Cedar Cottage and took a long, hot shower. The premises of the vacation rental were roomy, but not too large to take away from the cozy ambience. Since it was the off-season in the quaint beachside community, she'd gotten a week-to-week lease for a steal.

She dressed for a lazy day in a pair of yoga pants and a T-shirt. Afterward, she curled in front of the gas fireplace with a book in her lap, losing herself in the story.

A car door slammed in the distance. Deidre looked up, holding her breath. She heard the stomp of boots on the front steps, then a brisk knock at her door. The book she'd been reading slid heedlessly onto the couch cushion.

Somehow, she just knew it was Nick.

She hesitated for only a second before standing decisively.

"Hello. How are you?" he asked quietly, his gaze running over her face when she opened the door. He wore a pair of well-worn jeans and a hip-length black insulated jacket. He hadn't shaved today. Dark whiskers shadowed his jaw.

"Fine," Deidre replied warily.

He nodded, and she found herself shifting on her feet in the awkward silence that followed. Realizing she couldn't stand there forever with the door wide open, she reluctantly waved her hand into the kitchen. Nick entered. She shut the door and faced him.

"I drove around Harbor Town a little. It's nice. You must have loved coming here as a kid."

She attempted a smile. "Winter isn't the best time to be here. Harbor Town is a beach town, pure and simple."

He nodded. "It's still charming, decked out for the holidays like it is. I remember once when we were both with Linc you told him Christmas was your favorite holiday."

She blinked in surprise. She didn't remember ever having said such a thing in his presence. It made her feel exposed that he'd recalled the trivial detail.

"It was a favorite holiday when I was a child," she admitted. Longing ripped through her unexpectedly when she thought of Christmases when she was a kid—back in the days when she never doubted she was a true Kavanaugh. It was stupid, of course. She could return to her mother's house anytime—this very second if she chose. Her refusal to go there was a self-imposed sanction.

She looked up reluctantly when he placed a gloved finger beneath her chin and lifted it. She couldn't avoid his eyes now.

"Are you sure you're okay?"

She merely nodded, her throat convulsing uncomfortably when she swallowed.

His gaze moved over her face. "Why don't we go into the living room? It might be a little warmer?" he suggested, nodding toward the interior of the cottage.

"All right," she conceded.

She studied him while he removed his gloves and coat and draped his coat on the back of a kitchen chair. When he wasn't dressed in a suit, he favored jeans and shirts that weren't the classic cowboy variety, perhaps, but still possessed a Western flavor. They usually had snaps instead of buttons and fitted his lean, muscular torso to perfection.

When he glanced at her, she just raised her eyebrows in polite expectation, hoping he hadn't noticed the way she'd been detailing his form. She led him into the living room. The sitting area before the flickering fire looked much more cozy and intimate than it had when she'd been there alone.

"Did Lincoln ever speak to you about whether or not you were interested in running DuBois Enterprises?" he asked after he'd stood before the fire for a moment.

"Yes."

He turned and speared her with his stare. "He did? When?"

She shrugged. "I don't know. A month or so before he passed? He asked me if I'd ever consider taking up business. Then he asked me if I'd like to run his company. I thought he was kidding."

"And what did you say?" Nick asked intently.

"I told him 'no way.' I have no interest in working in an

office. Medicine is my career. I love being a nurse. Did Lincoln really ask you to get to know me better in that letter?" she blurted out, unable to contain her curiosity anymore. She'd been obsessing about Lincoln's reasoning and state of mind all day.

"Yes. Why would I lie about something like that?"

She gave him a small, cautious grin. "Your reasoning escapes me, as usual."

He laughed and turned toward her, one hand on the mantel. His silvery-gray eyes looked a little softer than usual. "My reasons are hardly Machiavellian."

"I just can't comprehend why he'd ask you to do it."

"Maybe he trusted me. Maybe you should, too."

She looked up into his face. He hadn't moved, but he somehow seemed closer. "Why should I trust you when you clearly don't trust me?"

"I haven't decided yet whether I trust you or not," he said.

A thought occurred to her. "Wait…don't tell me that *Lincoln* actually asked you to investigate me in this infamous letter."

"I'm not *investigating* you, Deidre. Don't be so melodramatic," he mumbled, exasperated.

"What else should I call it? You've admitted you're here to determine if I'm the type of person who would coerce a sick, vulnerable man into giving me all his money."

He sighed. "I'm here to understand you—and this whole situation—better. Linc's impulsive actions don't make much sense to me, given what I know of his character. He was an astute, methodical businessman. In order for me to get comfortable with the change, I need to get the lay of the land, so to speak. Linc's request for me to get to know you has nothing to do with my concerns about the will. It's a completely separate issue." He turned toward the fire, clutching at the edge of the mantel with both hands.

"I still think it's strange for you to stay in Harbor Town."

"Just as strange as Lincoln giving half the control of his entire company to a woman who probably can't even interpret a basic financial statement?" he wondered, giving her a steely sidelong glance.

Her spine stiffened. "Do you know what I think? I think it bothers you that Lincoln liked me so much."

"Why should it bother me that he was so taken by you? I suspect many men are," he said, holding her stare.

Her heart skipped a beat. She wasn't sure whether to interpret his comment as an insult or a compliment. "Maybe it bothers you because you're used to being the only one who had Lincoln's complete affection and trust."

He made a scoffing sound. "Linc gave his trust to many people, Deidre. Some of the officers of DuBois Enterprises thought he gave it a little too freely for their liking."

"As in my case, I suppose."

"Yes…and one other notable case," he said quietly. She frowned, confused by his reference. He dropped one hand and stepped toward her, so that only a half a foot separated them. She held her ground and hoped he didn't notice her pulse throbbing at her throat.

"It's not an inevitability that we have to be enemies," he said.

"It's not inevitable that we have to be friends, either," she said, staring at his chest.

"We might be friends, Deidre. Lincoln thought we could be, anyway."

"You haven't decided yet if I'm worthy of the title though yet, have you?"

Despite her cool sarcasm, his nearness made her blood race. Something about his voice affected her for some reason, especially when he said her name. When she'd first heard him speak, she would have taken his accent for typical

Midwestern—blunt, clipped, no-nonsense. Every once in a while though, a slight twang would slide into the syllables, a glimmer of something that reminded her of horses grazing in the high desert of the American West, the stark, rugged mountains and clean alpine air that surrounded The Pines.

"Deidre?"

"Yes?" she asked uneasily, meeting his stare.

"I never got a chance to tell you I was sorry about Linc's passing. Whether or not you're his daughter, I don't know, but no one could spend night and day with a person for months like you did and not be affected by the loss. Lincoln was certainly affected by you."

"Did he tell you that?" She longed to hear his answer, to know every tiny morsel of information about the man who had been in her life for such a fleeting time.

Nick hesitated for a moment. "Yes," he finally admitted. "But he didn't have to. He couldn't take his eyes off you when you were in the room with him."

She smiled shakily, both warmed and saddened by his words.

"We hardly ever spoke privately while we were at Tahoe, so I also never got a chance to thank you for insisting Linc be taken back to the hospital for diagnostic testing. You were right in thinking something didn't match up with his presentation and the diagnosis of multiple strokes. Because of your recommendation, we found out Linc's dysfunction wasn't just from his strokes. He had a brain tumor. You were right about that all along."

The surge of grief that went through her gave her the strength she needed to face the fire, breaking his magnetic stare. She lifted her chin. "I guess you were always too busy being suspicious that I'm a conniving opportunist to thank me at The Pines."

"I've been thinking about that. Maybe you're right," he

conceded slowly. She glanced over at him in surprise. "Having Lincoln inform me that he had a daughter shook me up a bit. I've been trying to make sense of things, and I can see why you take me for a rude, single-minded jerk. Why don't you turn the tables on me? Ask me anything you like."

For a second, she just stared at him silently before she directed her gaze to the flames.

"How did you meet Lincoln?" she asked.

"I was paired up with him in a Big Brother program when I was eight years old. Who knows where I would have ended up if that hadn't happened? Prison, most likely. Let's see," he paused, his gaze focused elsewhere as he delved into his memories. "I would have been in my sixth foster home placement in two years when I first met Linc. That summer, he hired me as his stable boy. I worked for him, in one capacity or another, for the next thirty years of my life, the only exception being when I was on active duty with the air force."

Her gaze lingered on his lips for two heartbeats. It was a firm mouth. She could imagine him giving brisk orders with it…easily picture every instruction being followed to a T.

It was also a sensual mouth. She could just as easily imagine women following his every demand in the bedroom. A flicker of annoyance went through her at the thought, but so did a flash of heat.

"Where did you serve while you were in the military?"

"I moved around. Turkey, Iraq—Operation Southern Watch. I did a stint in Sierra Leone."

"Were you involved in Operation Silver Anvil?" she asked, referring to the European Joint Operations Task Force that evacuated hundreds of people out of Sierra Leone by plane after a bloody military coup d'état.

"Yeah."

She gave him a swift, assessing glance. "Are you a pilot?"

He nodded once. "Still am, for private purposes. I own

a Cessna that I use to get around the country for business. I flew it here, actually. I'm renting hangar space over at Tulip City Airport."

She smiled. She should have known. He matched the profile of an air force pilot perfectly: handsome, cocky, amazingly sure of himself. His raised brows told her he'd noticed her smug expression. She hurried to change the subject.

"What happened to your parents?"

"They were killed in a car accident when I was six."

Her head swung around. "That's horrible. I'm sorry."

He shrugged. "Unlike most people, I know you really do understand just how terrible it was."

She swallowed and stepped away from the heat. She'd never spoken with him about the circumstances of Derry Kavanaugh's death, or the fact that Derry had caused an accident killing three other people, altering the paths of a dozen or more lives forever.

"Did Lincoln tell you about Derry dying in a car crash?"

"No."

Something in his tone made suspicion flicker in her. "Oh…I see. The infamous private investigator told you." She shook her head, feeling more exhausted than angry when his level gaze confirmed the truth of her words.

"You left me little choice but to have him gather all the details of your history," Nick admitted. "You refused to talk to me about your past or tell me anything about you."

She bit her lower lip, repressing her typical urge to tell him her life was none of his business. The words sounded thin and hollow tonight. "I'm a little tired. It's been a long day," she said.

"You should eat. Why don't you let me take you out to dinner? Or we could order in."

"No," she said too abruptly. She blushed and hurried to

cover her rudeness. "I…I mean, I really couldn't eat much more. I'm stuffed from a big brunch at Jake's Place."

"Can I take you to dinner tomorrow night, then?"

She gave an exasperated sigh. "You just don't quit, do you?"

"I told you I was determined."

"Determined to investigate my character and motives, or to fulfill Lincoln's wishes?" she murmured quietly.

"There's no reason I can't do both at once," Nick said before he strode toward the kitchen. Deidre followed. While he was putting on his coat, he added, "I'll bring you a copy of the will when we have dinner tomorrow."

"Is it possible to get two copies? I want my brother Marc to look it over. He's an attorney. You could drop his copy off at the Starling Hotel front desk, if it'll make things easier for you. Marc and his family are staying there, too."

He nodded. She struggled to interpret his expression when he didn't move.

"I probably should admit something."

"What?" she asked.

"I'm here at Lincoln's request and because I need to understand better why Lincoln changed his will. But aside from that…I'm glad to have the opportunity to get to know you better."

She just stared at him with her mouth partially open, too amazed to speak. Was he saying what she *thought* he was saying? Unless he was testing her again—

"Get a good night's sleep," he said, interrupting her confused thoughts.

"I'll do my best," she replied automatically. He gave her one last glance before he turned away. He checked the lock on the door before he closed it quietly behind him.

It wasn't until later that she realized she hadn't objected to him assuming she'd have dinner with him tomorrow.

She lay in bed that night, wondering why she'd grown so discombobulated when Nick mentioned the death of his parents. The reason finally came to her; it was the knowledge of how much they had in common. They'd both served in the military. Both of them had lost parents in car wrecks. Both of them had loved Lincoln DuBois. Circumstances had made them both highly independent and self-sufficient people.

They were both loners. And while Deidre wasn't an orphan in the classic sense, she thought she might have more of an idea of the loneliness of the condition than the average person. She knew the feeling of being different, of never perfectly fitting in anywhere.

She squeezed her eyes shut and rolled on her side. After recognizing that shared bond with Nick, sleep was a long time coming.

A light snow was starting to fall when she left the house at eleven the next morning. She had plans to visit Marc, Mari and her adorable little niece and godchild, Riley, at the Starling Hotel.

She recalled how Nick had casually slipped into their conversation last night that they'd have dinner together that evening. Was she going to let him get away with his subtle manipulation to spend time with her, or would she avoid Cedar Cottage during the dinner hour? She honestly wasn't sure about her answer as she headed over to the Starling Hotel, hoping all the while she had no unexpected run-ins with Nick.

During lunch she spilled the news about the will to a stunned Marc and Mari.

After the meal, Mari, Riley and she wandered out into the festively decorated hotel lobby while Marc went to check for a fax from Chicago at the front desk.

"Will you come back to Harbor Town for Christmas?"

Deidre asked Mari. Each of them was holding on to one of Riley's pudgy hands to protect the china vases and glittering Christmas tree ornaments from the curious toddler's grasp.

Mari shook her head regretfully. "Marc is far too busy with his campaign. Plus, I have a concert Christmas Eve," Mari said, referring to Marc's bid for a U.S. Senate seat and her own job as a cellist for the Chicago Symphony Orchestra. "Besides, I think I have finally convinced Ryan to come to Chicago for Christmas. He's officially a civilian now, like you." Mari asked, referring to her older brother, who had been an air force pilot.

"He is? That's wonderful. I always thought I'd run into him while we were both on active duty, but I never did. Are Marc and Ryan getting along now?" Deidre asked.

Mari made a face and glanced down at Riley. Marc and Ryan used to be best friends when they were teenagers. The car wreck Derry had caused while he'd been intoxicated had cruelly taken Ryan and Mari's parents from them. Grief and anger had severed Marc and Ryan's friendship long ago. "I wouldn't say getting along, precisely," Mari whispered, as if she thought Riley shouldn't hear. "They behave politely enough, for my sake and for Riley's."

The two women shared a glance of compassion. It hurt to know that the old wound between the once close families still festered.

"Would you like to stay with us in Chicago for the holiday?" Mari asked, looking glad to change the painful topic.

"No. I'll just lie low here for a while, look over that job proposal you gave me."

"Are you really considering taking the job at the Family Center?" Mari wondered enthusiastically as they sat on a deep-cushioned velvet couch and Riley started to crawl all over them. The Family Center was an innovative program for community education and treatment of substance abuse.

Mari had started the center because of the heavy toll drunk driving had taken on her life.

"I don't know. I love the idea of the preventative project I told you about for returning vets with substance abuse issues related to PTSD and depression, and it seems like a wonderful place to work. I'm going over there tomorrow to have Colleen show me around. Afterward, I'm going to help Eric out with an unexpected rush of intake exams," Deidre said, referring to Colleen's physician boyfriend, Eric Reyes, whom Deidre strongly suspected would be her fiancé very soon. "The Family Center is running on a skeleton staff during the holiday season. I've kept my nursing license active in Michigan, so it worked out great."

"That's wonderful," Mari enthused, dark eyes sparkling with the excitement of future plans.

Deidre laughed. "Don't plan on writing me a paycheck yet. I feel like I'm being tossed around by fate at the moment. My future seems so uncertain right now."

She suddenly realized that if Nick didn't contest the will, she'd be in a position to fund the project at the Family Center and many more like it. Funny, she'd never really thought of that possibility until now. It just all seemed so unlikely, so incongruous. *She*—a billionaire.

"Deidre? Are you okay?" Mari asked.

She blinked, realizing she was frowning. She laughed and kissed Riley's cheek when the little girl crawled into her lap and used Deidre's shoulders to pull herself into a standing position. Riley squealed and giggled when Deidre gave her a big hug. She'd never been so flattered and moved in her life when Marc and Mari had asked her to be the little girl's godmother. They'd even made Riley's middle name the same as Deidre's.

"I'm sorry," she said, bouncing Riley on her knee. "I'm really not myself lately."

"Understandable," Mari soothed. "You're life has been turned upside down within a matter of months. You should take some time off for rest and reflection. But I'm still thinking about Christmas. Will you go to Brigit's?" she asked delicately. "I know how much she wants you to come."

Deidre sighed, guilt and defiance sweeping through her in equal measure. She was growing increasingly familiar with the feeling, since she had experienced it in distilled form every time she'd noticed her mother had called her cell phone yesterday. She'd left every call unanswered. "I don't know. Maybe," Deidre murmured noncommittally. In truth, she wasn't sure what she'd do for Christmas. She didn't know if she was ready to return to the Kavanaugh house on Sycamore Avenue or to make amends with Brigit.

Marc joined them a minute later. He held up an envelope.

"Lincoln DuBois's will," he told Deidre. "I guess Nick Malone dropped it off at the front desk while we were at lunch. I'll look it over, then have a friend of mine who specializes in estate law go over it with a fine-tooth comb. I'll get back to you as soon as possible."

"That'd be great. Thank you, Marc."

Marc eyed her worriedly. "Please don't agree to anything Nick asks of you until you talk it over with me. I'm not crazy about leaving Harbor Town while he's here. I don't trust him. It's just our luck that Liam left town for his honeymoon the day after Malone arrived," Marc said, referring to Liam's job as the Harbor County police chief.

Deidre gave her brother a teasing grin. "There's no need for you to worry. Nick's presence here may be strange, but I hardly think he's going to resort to criminal activity."

"Do you have any interest whatsoever in running DuBois Enterprises?" Marc asked, his expression remaining serious.

"Look at it like this. If an alien landed in your front yard and asked you if you'd like to run their planet, what would you say? That's pretty much how I feel about this whole situation. I know absolutely nothing about business. Sure, I'd like to learn something about Lincoln's company, understand it better, but *run* it?" Deidre asked wryly, glancing from Marc to Mari.

"Just the fact that you're interested in DuBois Enterprises says something. Don't let Malone influence you. You're still in shock about everything that's happened to you. He might take advantage of that."

"Come on, Marc. You know as well as anyone I can take care of myself."

"We're talking about a hell of a lot of money here, and ten times as much power. It's not a world we're accustomed to, Dee. Who knows what people will do when the stakes are so high?"

Deidre laughed. "I said almost the exact same thing to Colleen yesterday." Her expression sobered as she studied her brother. "Marc—I'm worried about what could happen with your campaign if news gets out about the will. When things go public, there's a good chance the truth about Mom and Lincoln's affair, not to mention a lurid rehashing of the car crash, is going to show up in the papers. The Kavanaugh name could be dragged through the mud all over again."

Mari gave a small groan and looked at her husband anxiously. "I hadn't thought of that."

"It's not like the Kavanaughs haven't been on the receiving end of bad press before," Marc reminded both of them, pausing to stroke his wife's shoulder in reassurance. After Derry had caused the car wreck due to drunk driving, his name and reputation had been battered by the press. The Kavanaugh family had suffered by association. "As a matter of fact, my opponent in the Cook County prosecutor race brought up Dad's responsibility for the wreck, trying to use it for fuel. I'm used to mudslinging on the campaign trail."

"But it could ruin your chances for a win," Deidre protested.

Marc and Mari exchanged a significant glance.

"Marc's right," Mari said resolutely. "You have enough on your mind as it is without worrying about the outcome of Marc's race." When Marc swung his giggling daughter into his arms and changed the subject, Deidre took the hint and didn't belabor the topic, although she was far from being reassured.

She'd promised to pick up Liam and Natalie's mail while they were on their honeymoon in Turks and Caicos. By the time Deidre returned to Cedar Cottage later that afternoon, the snow had picked up. It wasn't enough to make conditions hazardous yet, but Deidre was glad to be getting home.

Would Nick show up here at the cottage to take her to dinner, she wondered as she went into the cottage. He hadn't called, but that wasn't too surprising, given the fact she'd never told him her number. She supposed she should, given their strange, probably impermanent partnership at DuBois Enterprises.

She took a hot bath and dressed in a pair of jeans and a favorite soft, cotton cable-knit sweater. To her dismay, she found herself spending way too much time on her makeup, accentuating the color and shape of her eyes with liner and subtle eye shadow. When she realized what she was doing, she irritably threw the makeup in a bag and stalked out of the bathroom.

What was she doing, primping for Nick Malone?

She was convinced she was indifferent to his arrival when a knock came at her door a little after six o'clock.

She was entirely uncaring about seeing him, that is, until she opened her front door and saw him standing on the dim porch, snow dusting his hair and jacket, and holding the trunk of a perfectly shaped, six-foot pine tree and a huge bag from Shop and Save.

"I thought you might like a Christmas tree," he stated simply.

She blinked in amazement, transferring her gaze from the tree to his face. She was stunned. Had he noticed last night—that flash of longing she'd tried to hide when they'd talked about childhood Christmases? Had he noticed months ago, at The Pines, when she'd conversed with Lincoln?

She *knew* he had when she looked into his somber eyes, knew it down in her very bones.

"I hope it's okay," he said quietly. "What do you say, Deidre? A truce? Just for one night?" he added when she didn't speak.

She dazedly realized she'd just left him standing there at the front door, gaping at him.

"I…well…all right. I mean…it *is* a great tree." His face lit up at her flustered response. She gave him a sheepish grin. It was hard to frown at Nick when he flashed those dimples.

He gave the pine a good shake to remove the few snow-flakes that had settled on the upper boughs.

"One of the reasons I got this one was that it was beneath a canopy and completely dry…at least until I carried it to the car," he explained, knocking off a last few stubborn flakes with his gloved hand.

Without thinking Deidre stepped forward and brushed snow off his shoulder, going up on tiptoe to swipe her hand through his dark brown hair. The strands felt thick, soft and chilled beneath her fingers. He glanced at her in surprise. His face was close. He had little flecks of black interspersed in the silver-gray of his irises. His lashes were very thick….

She cleared her throat and stepped back, banging her hip clumsily on the door.

"Come in," she said breathlessly, opening the door wider

to make way for Nick and his heartwarming gift, all the while hoping she wasn't making a huge mistake by letting him into the cottage…by inviting him into her life.

Chapter Three

They set the tree in the front window where it could be easily admired from the rural road and while curled up on the couch before the fire. Deidre busied herself pulling out all the decorations from the bag while Nick arranged the tree in the base.

"Look at these old-fashioned lights! I love these. They're so retro," she said, grinning as she withdrew large, colored bulbs from the bag. Nick removed his head from beneath the tree and glanced back at her. She couldn't help but notice he was awesome to look at, lying on his side with his back to her, his hands beneath the tree, tightening the screws on the base. His body was long, his hips were lean, his thighs strong-looking. His back muscles flexed interestingly beneath the blue-and-white plaid fitted shirt he wore. She dragged her gaze off the vision of his butt outlined in a pair of jeans.

Her cheeks heated when she noticed his strange expression. Had he noticed where she'd been staring?

"What's wrong?" she asked when he continued to look at her.

"Nothing. It's just—Lincoln liked that kind of bulb, too. He never gave a damn about new trends. Not when it came to Christmas. He put up an old-fashioned Christmas tree at The Pines—large, colored bulb lights, garland, tinsel...always the biggest, most gorgeous tree on the lake," he mumbled. He stuck his head beneath the tree again.

Deidre walked toward him, still holding the box of lights. "Would Lincoln have the staff put up the tree?"

"The staff helped, but Linc was always in the middle of things. He'd make a party of it," she heard him say from beneath the boughs. "Sasha, Linea, Otto and Linda joined us last year," he said, mentioning Lincoln's chef, administrative assistant, driver and one of his nurses. "Linc insisted on being brought downstairs and overseeing things from his wheelchair."

"So you were always there for the Christmas decorating ritual?" Deidre asked, running her fingers over the supple needles of the tree.

"Yeah, I usually made a point of trying to clear my schedule to be there."

She imagined the staff, Nick and Lincoln, the festive mood lightening their spirits, Lincoln directing them on their decorating and encouraging them to partake of food and drink. "Of course, you must have put the tree in front window of the great room. It must have looked fabulous."

"Yeah. Lincoln was like a kid at Christmastime. I wouldn't be surprised if he asked the architect to design The Pines with that huge window so that he could get himself a twenty-five-foot pine to put in it every year. How's that look? Is it straight?" he queried.

Deidre stepped back and walked in a half circle, inspecting the tree—and Nick—beneath it. "It's perfect."

He backed out and stood. She waved toward the kitchen. "I bought some hot chocolate earlier. It's just instant, but—"

"I'd love some."

"Oh…okay, great, then I'll just—"

"Here. I'll start to put on the lights and you get the hot chocolate," he said, coming toward her. She handed him the box of bulbs. When he didn't move back and Deidre didn't immediately head toward the kitchen, a strange combination of awareness of his nearness and awkwardness struck her at once.

"What about music?" he asked.

She started. "Music?"

"Yeah. You know…'White Christmas,' 'Jingle Bells.'"

Deidre laughed. She couldn't help it. Something about the idea of scowling, bottom-line, business-mogul Nick Malone getting into the Christmas spirit was funny, and yet…*right* somehow, too.

She ignored his bewildered expression at her laughter and walked toward the bedroom, where there was a radio. "I'll see if I can't find a station playing some.

"Was Lincoln responsible for this?" she mused a few minutes later when she walked into the living room with two steaming mugs. "We Three Kings" played softly on the radio while snow drifted down at a lazy pace outside of the window.

"For me bringing over the Christmas tree?" Nick asked as he strung on lights.

"No. For this unexpected proclivity for Christmas spirit in Nick Malone," she said, turning the handle of his mug so he could grasp it with one hand.

He took a sip, studying her from over the rim.

"You assumed I'd be a Scrooge, I guess."

"All I have to go on is precedent."

A shiver went through her at the sound of his deep, gravelly laughter.

"Maybe you're right," he said, handing the cup back to her after a moment. "I have a lot of really good memories from Christmases at The Pines. After we met, Linc invited me over every year for the decorating party and also on Christmas Eve. When I got older, he was always encouraging me to lighten up at that time of year…enjoy the holiday…try to reflect on what it was I was working so hard for. What about you?"

She set his mug on the mantel and glanced back at him. "What do you mean?"

He shrugged and resumed his task. "How'd you get to like Christmas so much?"

"My family was always big on Christmas," Deidre said, poking through the bag and beginning to unwrap some garland. "Although as a kid, I might have been the most avid Kavanaugh Christmas devotee." She glanced up to see his gaze was on her face even as his hands moved in the branches. "I adored Christmastime. It was just…" She shrugged sheepishly. "Magical."

He said nothing as he continued to string on the lights, but she didn't have the impression of being dismissed for her whimsy.

"You're really going to miss Lincoln, aren't you?" she asked softly after a moment. He paused in his actions and met her stare.

"Yeah," he said. "I really am."

Deidre admitted to herself that Nick had known her guard would be breached by the gift of the Christmas tree. She should have been alarmed by that knowledge. But it was difficult to think of him as her enemy as they sat on the couch, admiring the pretty, glowing tree they'd decorated together while snow fell outside the window. A big band rendition of

"Winter Wonderland" played on the radio and the fire kept the room toasty.

Her respect for him grew as she drew him out about his work at DuBois Enterprises. Lincoln had informed her that Nick was a brilliant business leader—instinctively knowing when to strike aggressively, but also understanding when caution and restraint were required. Nick clearly considered himself a servant to the larger cause of a healthy, vibrant business.

The truth was, she was having a nicer time than she'd experienced in years spending the evening with Nick. He could potentially turn on her tomorrow. She would fight him if he tried to contest the will on the grounds that she'd coerced Lincoln. She didn't want to run DuBois Enterprises, but she refused to have Nick sully the fact that Lincoln had believed heart and soul she was his child. Lincoln's revised will was tangible proof of that. She couldn't let Nick take that from her.

She wouldn't.

Maybe she was being foolish by not fighting him tonight. Maybe she was being weak. But maybe she just really needed a nice evening with an intelligent, attractive, sexy man.

Even if that man was Nick Malone.

She asked him about the acquisition deal he'd mentioned on the first night he'd come to Harbor Town. He filled her in on the details. The owner of a media company called Vivicor, Inc., had been toying with the idea of selling to DuBois for months now. Nick liked the company's price and earning potential and wanted to expand DuBois Enterprises's market share in media. He'd been wooing the owner for close to a year. However, Vivicor was a family-owned company and the president was wavering. Just after Lincoln had died, Nick had received a call from the owner that he was ready to sell on the original terms.

"I'd like to strike while the iron is hot. The owner has

been known to stall in the past," Nick explained as he held up the carton of lemon chicken, offering her more. Deidre shook her head. They'd ordered Chinese and talked almost nonstop as they ate, both of them avoiding potentially volatile topics like Lincoln's will or the genetic testing. Deidre thought Nick would pursue the topic of acquiring Vivicor, Inc., angling for her agreement to complete the deal, but to her surprise, he changed the subject.

Who knew? Deidre wondered as she watched Nick spoon the last of the lemon chicken onto his plate. Maybe Nick had needed a truce and a nice evening as much as she had.

"Did you ever do what Lincoln requested?" she asked a few minutes later as she sank back into the couch and brought her feet up next to her. "Did you ever reflect on what it was you work so hard for, day in and day out?" she clarified when he arched his brows at her. He gave her a sidelong glance as he chewed. She enjoyed observing the movement of his strong jaw.

"I've reflected," he said finally, wiping his mouth with a napkin and setting his plate on the table.

"And? Any grand discoveries?"

"No. Not really," he admitted, leaning back after he took a swig of ice water. "I was different than Linc in that way. The work has always been reason and reward enough for me. It was Linc who was worried he'd built up his empire for nothing, that it was a hollow victory. 'What's it all for?' he'd ask me every once in a while."

"Was he unhappy?" Deidre asked in a hushed tone.

He met her gaze. "No. I would say he lived a happy, fulfilled life. But everyone has a sore point. For Linc, it was that he'd never had a family with whom he could share all that he had to give."

Deidre studied her thighs, blinking to soothe the sudden

burn in her eyes. *Oh, no.* She really wished these tears would be over and done with.

Her breath caught when she felt Nick touch the juncture between her neck and shoulders. His long fingers combed through her hair. He didn't speak, but she knew he'd noticed her emotional upsurge. She felt like she needed to explain.

"It's just…it's hard, knowing he wanted a family so much and didn't know he had one all along."

Didn't know he had me.

The thought of both Linc and her having similar longings while separated by half of the world, both ignorant of each other's existence, made grief spike through her. They'd found each other, but for such a brief time. Now he was gone forever.

She stared at the flames and muffled a sob. A hot, vivid flash of anger at her mother mingled with her sadness. Her wretchedness was so complete in that moment, she didn't protest when she felt Nick's arms surround her. She managed to stifle the sound of her misery, but she couldn't disguise the tremors that racked her body. Nick didn't comment, just absorbed her sadness, his body seeming to cushion the impact of her grief.

She realized she'd never really wept since Lincoln died. Nick cradled her waist and encouraged her to rest the back of her head on his chest. He ran his hand along her shoulder and upper arm. For several minutes, she cried silently while she stared at the fire.

Nick closed his hand over her shoulder muscle and rubbed it. She felt his heat through the tiny holes of her sweater. She held her breath. Awareness of him, of his closeness, of his hard, male body made her misery fade. His hand stilled, as if he'd recognized the alteration in her mood at the same moment she had.

She stood abruptly from the couch and grabbed a napkin

from the table. She wiped off her cheeks and walked toward the mantel. How crazy could she be, going to mush like that in front of a man who doubted she was Lincoln's daughter, who doubted her morals and her character?

"Surely Lincoln didn't grieve that much over not having a family," she said flatly as she leaned down toward the flames, her back to Nick. "He had you, after all."

"I worked for him, Deidre."

"He loved you like a son," she insisted. "Everyone says so. He positively glowed with pride every time he spoke of you. Why can't you admit you thought of him like a father?"

When he didn't speak, she twisted her chin over her shoulder, feeling regretful at her outburst. Had she sounded bitter just then? She'd accused him last night of being envious of her relationship with Lincoln, but perhaps she was the one who was jealous of Nick's lifelong association with Lincoln. She didn't know what to think when she saw the way he studied her, his face impassive, his eyes hooded.

"I won't admit it, because it's not true. I never expected Lincoln to treat me as his son. I worked my ass off for him—as a stable boy, as the foreman of his ranch, as an advertising executive, as a new global unit president and finally as his CEO."

"I didn't mean you'd taken advantage of your relationship with him," she said, caught off guard.

"Other people thought so, when I was younger," he stated bluntly. "Maybe that's why I was so intent on making sure my work spoke for itself. I never wanted to give anyone the slightest reason to suspect that I'd used Linc. My record stands on its own."

Deidre blushed. She hadn't realized it was such a sensitive topic for him. Of course, what he'd said made complete sense. There would always be those who thought the worst of a person's motives.

"When I told you last night that the officers of DuBois Enterprises had been known to think Linc was foolish for putting so much trust in another human being," Nick continued, "I was talking about myself. There was loads of backbiting and plenty of rumors about Linc's gullibility when I first started working for him and rising in the ranks."

She stared at him, her lips parted in amazement.

"Maybe you're thinking it's pretty damn hypocritical of me to sit here and say that I was accused of taking advantage of Lincoln when I was young, and then turn around and do the same to you," he said quietly. "But it's different, Deidre."

"How?"

"Because I *did* build a record of service to Linc, his company and it's employees. I silenced all the naysayers, many times over."

"How am I supposed to compete with that, Nick?" she asked, frustrated.

"I'm not asking you to. All I'm asking is that you spend time with me, allow me to get to know you…form my own opinions."

"Haven't I been doing that tonight?"

"Yeah, you have. And I appreciate it. More than you know."

Deidre wondered if she'd ruined their peaceful evening with her emotional outburst when he suddenly stood.

"I'm sorry," she said. "I didn't mean to sound so angry—"

"Don't apologize. I'm not leaving. I just thought of something, that's all. It arrived yesterday." She stared at him, bewildered, when he waved at the front door. "I'll go and get it. It's in the car."

Her confusion had only amplified by the time he returned a minute later, carrying an opened cardboard shipping box. Deidre hurried to finish clearing the coffee table of the remnants of their dinner, making room for him to set it down.

"What is it?" she asked a moment later when she'd returned from the kitchen, her eyes glued to the box.

"Open it," he encouraged.

She knelt next to the table while he sat across from her on the couch. She peeled back the box flaps and peered inside, seeing dozens and dozens of black-and-white and color photos. Excitement pulsed through her. She reached for the five-by-six photo of a woman smiling at the camera, an exquisite arrangement of white hydrangeas and roses on the table before her, sunlight flooding through the window behind her.

Recognition clicked in her, rapid and absolute.

"It's Lily DuBois," she whispered.

"Let me see," Nick requested gruffly.

She turned the photo. He gave a small smile.

"Yeah. That's Lily."

"You knew her?" Deidre whispered.

He nodded. "I knew both Lily and George, Linc's father. George was a rancher. He owned a huge spread between Tahoe and Carson City. When they got older, Lincoln bought a house for them in South Lake, and they spent most of their time there."

"What were they like?" Deidre asked as she withdrew another picture, this one of Lily in the arms of a large, sun-tanned man with silver-gray hair and a winning smile. She studied every nuance of the couple's faces, hungry for the tiniest details. Lily and George DuBois—*her grandparents*.

"The two of them couldn't have been more different, but they were perfect for each other. George was a lot like Linc, bigger than life, personable, a natural horseman, smart and methodical when it came to business. Lily was reserved. Elegant. A sweeter lady never lived. She was English, did Linc tell you that?"

Deidre nodded, now studying Nick like she had the photographs, so eager for any tiny morsel of knowledge about people and a history she'd never known.

"Lily never lost her accent. It made her seem so refined, but never standoffish. Her warmth was her hallmark. She loved flowers and used to show her roses in competitions. The one thing both Lily and George had in common was the love of the land. Lily was always in her garden, George with his horses."

Deidre continued to dig through the photographs, peering at the faces of people she'd never known, but who somehow seemed familiar to her. There were photos of Lincoln as a young man, tall and whipcord lean, deeply tanned from his days working on his father's ranch. She saw Lily working in her garden, always wearing a white straw hat to protect her skin from the sun.

"Here's a picture of one of Linc's Christmas trees," Nick said a few minutes after he'd begun to join her in examining the photos.

Deidre came around the table and sat next to him on the couch. There was the magnificent pine tree arranged in the picture window of the great room of The Pines. Standing before it was Lincoln, perhaps at around forty, looking fit, handsome and happy. Next to him stood his mother and father. George had his arm around a tall young man, wearing jeans and a sober expression.

"That's you," Deidre whispered as she studied the image of a teenage Nick. He'd been very handsome and intense, even as a boy. A strange feeling went through her, seeing Nick standing there with Lincoln's family—*her* family. "What were you so serious about?"

Nick frowned at the photograph, his brows forming a V shape. "Who knows? I probably was worried about getting my homework done or something," he said dryly.

"Homework?" Deidre laughed. "You were that serious about your schoolwork? How come?"

"I think I'm about sixteen in the photo. I was trying to get a scholarship for college," he said, shrugging.

"Wouldn't Lincoln have helped you with college?"

"He would have. I didn't want him to," he said in a clipped tone that made Deidre realize she was once again treading on tender territory. He must have realized how he'd sounded because he waved his hand sheepishly. "It was a thing between Linc and me. He always wanted to give me more than I was willing to take. He would have taken over as my foster parent at any time, but I…"

"What?" Deidre prompted.

He shrugged. "I was stubborn. I resisted the idea, for some reason. Linc offered to adopt me, as well, but I told him no. I ended up making peace with the Garritsons—the family that fostered me and three other boys—until I went to college. It's ironic, I guess, how I rebelled against foster families when I was a kid and then finally accepted a family because I didn't want Linc to take me."

"I don't understand. You and Lincoln got on so well together."

He glanced at her sharply. "I didn't want to rely on his generosity. I didn't have much of anything as a kid but a huge chip on my shoulder that might loosely—*very* loosely—have been called pride," he said with a wry smile. "I spent most of my time at The Pines. I thought of it as home, but I always kept that barrier between Linc and me. I wanted to prove I was worthy of every opportunity he gave me, and it's hard to do that if you're legally lord of the manor, if you know what I mean. I'd like to think he understood my need for independence and to prove myself, but I'm not so sure he did. He would tell me I was too serious and needed to enjoy my youth while I still had it. It was an ongoing refrain between the two of us. Just a few days before he passed, he was admonishing me for working night and day on a merger deal."

"He wanted you there with him. He likely suspected the end was coming," Deidre murmured, carefully placing the photograph on the table and leaning back on the couch, her gaze on his profile.

"He was right. I should have been with him every minute instead of on the phone, worrying about meaningless business details. I regret it now," he said stiffly.

"You couldn't have known precisely when his last days would be. You were there when the time came. You said your goodbyes. It's normal to regret things when people we love pass," she said softly. "We always wish we'd done and said more."

His gaze narrowed on her. Deidre wondered what he saw on her face. "Was this a bad idea?" he asked, nodding toward the table that was now littered with photos.

She self-consciously wiped at a damp cheek. "No. It was a wonderful idea. Thank you for having the photos sent. Why did you?"

"Why did I what?" His longish bangs had fallen on his forehead. Deidre suppressed and urge to comb the strands back with her fingers. How could he seem so hard and cold at times and all too human and approachable at others? A spell seemed to have fallen over her as she tried to gauge his reaction to the photos and understand his relationship to Lincoln. She saw him differently tonight than she had before. He felt deeply about Lincoln, but he rarely spoke of his feelings. It was as if he didn't think he had a right to have such strong emotions toward Lincoln.

Did he possibly resent her showing up at the last moments of Lincoln's life, claiming to be his flesh and blood daughter? It saddened her to consider it, but she could completely understand if he did feel that way. She wished for the tenth time that evening that the circumstances between Nick and her weren't so unusual, so tense, so inherently ridden with conflict. He was a complex, interesting man.

"Why did you have the photographs sent, when you're not even convinced I'm Lincoln's daughter?" she clarified softly.

The silence seemed to swell. Deidre experienced his gaze moving over her face like a physical touch. His nostrils flared slightly when his stare landed on her mouth.

"I thought Linc would have wanted you to see them."

"Oh...I see."

He looked into her eyes. "I'm not so sure that you do."

She swallowed thickly. They'd started talking in hushed, intimate voices. She couldn't unglue her stare from his moving lips.

He lowered his head until their faces were just inches apart. He opened his hand along the side of her head. She trembled when she felt him moving his fingers through her hair. "Why didn't you tell me about the genetic testing?" he asked, his breath fanning her lips.

"I don't know," she admitted. "I was mad at you for always pushing it. I was scared—"

"Don't be afraid," he cut her off in a pressured tone. His hand came around and cradled her jaw. "I can understand you being angry, but don't be scared. Not of me. Not ever."

She heard his voice through the pounding of her heart in her ears. She watched him, entranced by his image. He looked intent...fierce.

"There's something I've been wanting to do ever since I laid eyes on you."

"What?" she whispered.

"This."

He covered her mouth with his own.

Something had clenched tight in Nick's chest when De-idre said the word *scared*. She looked sublimely beautiful staring up at him, her head cradled in his hand, her pink lips parted like a lush, blooming rose.

He shouldn't have brought over the photos. It'd been insensitive of him. He wasn't sure if Deidre was Lincoln's biological child, but he'd come to the conclusion after spending the evening with her that *she* believed it, heart and soul. She believed Lincoln, Lily and George were the family she'd never known. It must have been brutal for her to see them all alive and happy, to witness the evidence of all the days, months and years of lives she'd never known, and never would.

His concern for her vulnerability didn't silence his mounting desire for her. In fact, it seemed to be increasing it. An overwhelming need to protect her rose in him, mingling with an even more powerful mandate to devour her...possess her. He could have resisted her delicious-looking mouth as easily as he could have single-handedly turned night to day.

Her lips were as eager as his. It enflamed him, the way she leaned into him, the way she molded and shaped her flesh to his, the way she tasted. He slid his tongue along the seam of her lips, hungry for more of her unique flavor. When he probed into the center of her warmth, and she opened for him so willingly, a groan burned in his throat.

She was sweetness distilled.

He probed the cavern of her mouth, stroking, caressing, seeking out more of her secrets. His other hand came up to cradle her jaw. He held her in place, his entire being focused on a kiss that was damned near singeing his very consciousness it was so hot.

She slid her tongue against his and applied a suction that he felt all the way to the place he burned hottest. He muttered her name as he bit at her plump lower lip and then captured her mouth again in a searing kiss. She ran her fingers through his hair, her touch causing a shudder of pleasure to course through him. His hands settled on her shoulders. He brought her against him, suppressing a growl of primal satisfaction at how supremely good she felt. She arched her back and her breasts pressed against his ribs.

He broke the kiss and gritted his teeth.

"You've been driving me crazy since I first laid eyes on you," he whispered roughly as he kissed her neck. It was true. He'd been consumed with a desire to touch her from the first moment she'd looked at him with those singular blue-gray eyes and tilted her chin up in that part amused, part defiant gesture she favored. Her skin was so smooth it was like pressing his lips against a fragrant flower petal. Her body seemed to flow beneath his seeking hands, sleek muscle, supple, tight curves—the perfect combination of strength and soft femininity. He pressed his lips against her throbbing pulse.

"Your heart is beating so fast." He slid his hand along her chest and rested it over her left breast. She stilled. Her heart pulsed against his palm. Her eyes were glassy with desire when he lifted his head, her lips rosy and damp from his kiss. A primitive, powerful urge rose in him to make love to her.

He shouldn't do it. Things were getting out of hand. It would make things messy when what he most needed in this venture was objectivity.

She parted her lips.

To hell with objectivity.

He seized her mouth with his own.

He urged her to lie on her back on the couch and came down over her, never breaking their kiss. His blood rushed hot and fast through his veins. One thing existed in the universe for him at that moment, and for once, it wasn't his drive to make a shrewd business decision.

Only Deidre mattered—only that, and the overwhelming need to lose himself in her.

Chapter Four

He pressed kisses along the top of her sweater-covered breasts while she raked her fingers through his hair. Her touch drove him crazy. There was too much clothing separating them. He reached for the bottom of her sweater, pausing when he heard Deidre whimper. He let the material fall from his hand at the poignant sound.

He lifted his head, spearing her with his stare.

"What is it?"

"I can't, Nick," she whispered. "It's not right. You don't trust me."

It was on the tip of his tongue to deny it, to say his trust in her grew the more time he spent with her. He stopped himself when he realized how it would sound if he uttered those words.

She'd think he was saying it just to get her into bed.

He cursed under his breath and sat up. It felt like ripping off his own skin to separate himself from her warm, soft, supple body. He clamped his eyes shut and raked his fingers through his hair.

"You don't trust me either," he muttered. "It was a mistake not to spend more time with you while Linc was still alive."

"You were busy. And when you were at The Pines, I wouldn't let you spend time with me," she said as she sat up. Her low, smoky voice seduced him all over again. He glanced back at her, sorely tempted to touch her again…to draw her close. Her eyes looked huge in her delicate face. She wrapped her arms beneath her breasts, hugging herself. He was reminded of her vulnerability.

"Will you let me now?" he asked. "For more than just tonight?"

Her serious expression cut at him a little. "I'll try," she whispered, her eyes never leaving his face.

"Thank you for a nice night."

She nodded once. "Thank you for the Christmas tree and photos."

He was having difficulty pulling his gaze off her face.

"I don't want to dislike you," she said with sudden earnestness. "It doesn't seem right. Especially now that I'm starting to understand how much you meant to Lincoln."

He closed his eyes and glanced away.

"Nick?" she whispered.

"Yeah," he muttered, inhaling deeply and willing his boiling blood to cool.

"That company, Vivicor? Do you really think it's important that you—we—move fast on the purchase?"

He glanced back at her in surprise. "Yes."

She looked hesitant. "If you think it's a good business decision, I'll do whatever you want me to do to make the deal happen. I don't want to hold back progress in Lincoln's company."

A silence ensued. She seemed hesitant in meeting his stare. "Are you sure, Deidre?"

She nodded, although she looked far from certain to him. "Because I don't want you ever thinking that what happened just now—" he waved at the couch they'd come close to incinerating with sudden, blazing need "—had anything to do with me getting your agreement for the Vivicor purchase or DuBois Enterprises or the will."

"I don't think that." Her expression didn't entirely convince him that what she said was true, though.

He sighed and rubbed his eyes with his fingers. The thought struck him that there was a good chance family members had warned her against him, advised her not to sign anything he requested, and here she was, offering to do just that. No wonder she looked so uncertain. He couldn't say he blamed her.

But damn it, he *did* need her consent for the deal.

"Why don't you give me your phone number and we'll get together tomorrow afternoon and go over things in more detail. You can make your decision about Vivicor then," he said, standing. They walked to the kitchen, and he donned his coat. She stood watching him, the flush of arousal on her cheeks a stark contrast to the paleness of the rest of her skin. He fought down another surge of desire to take her into his arms again.

"Trust takes time, Deidre."

"I know that," she said quickly.

"I mean in the literal sense, not just the figurative. The more time we spend with each other, the more comfortable we'll be."

"As business partners?"

"As any kind of partner."

He touched her cheek before he opened the front door,

and experienced the strangest mixture of triumph and utter defeat as he walked into the frigid December night.

Deidre couldn't sleep. So much had changed between Nick and her that night, it was a challenge to wrap her mind around it all. The memories of the evening that made her most restless were of that kiss—the way Nick's mouth felt moving over hers, his taste, his lean, solid body pressed against hers, his heat…

She finally fell asleep just before dawn. When she awoke to the jarring sound of the alarm, all of her doubts and uncertainties were there, ready to pounce on her. She rose, wishing she hadn't promised Colleen and Eric she'd help out at the Family Center today. She was exhausted. For more days in a row now than she could recall, she put an extra scoop of coffee in her morning brew.

She'd responded wholeheartedly to Nick's touch, she admitted to herself bemusedly as she showered. She'd known there was a spark of attraction between them, but their suspicion of one another and the strange circumstances had made it necessary to suppress that spark. Attraction was one thing, but the degree of heat Nick and she had generated when they touched was unprecedented, at least in Deidre's experience. She'd been one kiss, one stroke, one plea away from going to bed with Nick Malone, of all people.

Surely she was behaving predictably, falling for such an attractive, powerful man. Most women would have adored spending an evening with him, basking in his attention and blossoming beneath his masterful kiss. Problem was, Deidre wasn't most women. And the situation between them was far from common.

Bizarre, more like it.

Had she made the wrong choice, allowing him into her life?

No clear-cut answer came to her soul-searching, and she finally resolved to live with the uncertainty. Of course it hadn't been wrong to consent to the Vivicor acquisition when Nick—a brilliant businessman—endorsed it wholeheartedly.

He'd been right about the issue of trust. It would come if it was meant to come, but in its own time.

Work and the familiar routine of her nursing duties acted as a godsend to her stormy spirit. She enjoyed Colleen's tour of the Family Center and working with Eric on intake exams. Afterward, she drove through Harbor Town, feeling reflective.

She drove past Sutter Park, seeing the town's festive Christmas tree and the kids ice-skating in the outdoor rink. It wasn't a familiar sight to her. Liam and Colleen had been full-time Harbor Towners for a period of time in their youth, attending high school there following Derry's death. Marc and Deidre, however, had spent only their childhood summers in the picturesque lakeside community. Maybe being there in the wintertime was partially responsible for this discordant feeling she possessed, like she was returning home, but also a stranger in Harbor Town.

Her mother wanted this to be a homecoming. Deidre had lost count of the number of calls she'd left unanswered from Brigit Kavanaugh. Maybe their mother-daughter rift was responsible for her present feeling of nostalgia and loss.

Wanting to snap herself out of her gloomy mood, Deidre parked at the Starling Hotel. Marc, Mari and Riley were leaving later that afternoon for Chicago. She'd already said her goodbyes yesterday, but seeing her brother and his family one more time would be a dose of good medicine.

She walked along the plush carpet, her attention fracturing when she heard a man speak from one of half a dozen private alcoves branching off the luxurious main lobby of the hotel. She came to an abrupt halt, recognizing the voice.

Nick sat in an armed, wingback chair that angled away from Deidre as she approached, his long, jean-covered legs sprawled before him. Deidre could only see him in partial profile. She walked toward him, excitement and anxiety at the unexpected encounter making her heart thud rapidly.

"The important thing is that she's seeing the importance of being more cooperative. No, we won't get any of those results for a week or more," he said.

Deidre paused in her silent tread on the plush carpet, realizing his cell phone was pressed to his ear and that he was in the middle of a conversation. She hesitated, preparing to retrace her steps to give him privacy.

"You're not going to get them to speed up the results any, John. Confidentiality is crucial in the health care field," Nick said.

John. He must be speaking to John Kellerman, DuBois Enterprises's chief legal officer, she thought as she eased backward. Kellerman had never tried to disguise his contempt for Deidre.

"I told you yesterday where I stand on the matter. I've witnessed nothing so far to even hint she had any part in coercing him to change his will."

Deidre stopped dead in her tracks. Nick was talking about *her.*

"According to her, she had no idea Linc had plans to alter his will," he said, then paused, listening. He straightened in the chair. "I'll do what's best for DuBois Enterprises. You know that... No, *I'm* the one who has to be satisfied, John. Not you. I'm the one whose interest and shares were decreased by the new will. As the injured party, I'm the only one who can legally contest the will, if it should ever come to that," Nick said, his voice quiet but sleety with anger. He paused. "I recognize it might not have been the wisest choice Lincoln could have made for the company. Lincoln's state of mind when he changed the will is a separate issue from whether or not Deidre Kavanaugh is truly his daughter and whether or not she had any part in manipulating him to change his will in her favor. I'm inclined to doubt the latter. We'll just have to wait for the lab results. As for the rest, I'm not certain what to think yet."

A man and a woman passed in the lobby behind her conversing loudly. Deidre hardly noticed as she listened to Nick talk about her as coolly as he might the daily stock market news.

"No. Deidre told me the name of the facility. GenLabs, in Carson City," Nick said.

Deidre inhaled sharply. Nick sat forward abruptly, his gaze latching on her. She turned and rushed toward the lobby exit.

"Deidre…wait!"

She ignored his command and hurried toward the front doors, stumbling when she crashed into a man entering the lobby while talking on his cell phone. She mumbled an apology and soared out of the hotel toward the parking lot. Just before she slammed her car door shut, she heard Nick call out to her again. She ignored him, her brain awash with anxiety over what she'd just heard.

By adding me to his will, Lincoln cut Nick's inheritance? she thought numbly. Nick had just mentioned the genetic testing to Nick Kellerman so coldly, as though something that had become crucially important to her very identity was a business factoid to be shared and bartered.

She'd made a mistake by being honest with him. Thank *goodness* she hadn't yet broken her word to Marc and signed anything at Nick's request. By the time she pulled into Cedar Cottage's drive, her heart was beating a rapid, furious tempo against her breastbone. She sat gripping the wheel for half a minute after she shut off the car, trying to calm herself, willing the queasiness in her belly to diminish. Again, her appetite had been poor this morning, and now she was paying for it. She opened the car door, gulping in the cold, fresh air coming off the lake.

"Deidre."

She swayed next to her car, glancing back. Nick was getting out of his sedan. She'd been so disoriented she hadn't noticed him pull in behind her. He was coatless, and his expression was tense.

He slammed his car door shut and stalked toward her. Something volatile felt like it was going to explode from her chest. She raced through the yard and up the front steps of Cedar Cottage, nearly making it to her front door when Nick caught her elbow. She spun around and yanked at her arm, but he held firm. Words burst out of her throat like she'd been storing them under pressure.

"I can't believe you told him about the testing! I told you that in confidence."

"You never asked me to keep it a secret, Deidre," Nick said, towering over her.

She struggled to inhale. She felt like she'd been slugged back in that lobby and she was still recovering from that blow.

"Why didn't you tell me that Lincoln had cut your shares in DuBois and his inheritance to you when he included me in the will?"

"I wasn't trying to keep it from you," he said, vapor from his breath billowing around his mouth. "I thought it would have been obvious, that I was previously his sole heir."

A tear of frustration and anger landed on her cheek, seeming to freeze against her skin. "A lot of things aren't obvious to me, Nick. You've accused me in the past of taking advantage of Lincoln when he was vulnerable, and yet you have no problem at all doing the same to me. You know I don't know very much about business. You know I'm…confused after everything that has happened to me in the past few months," she said furiously. "I let down my guard to you last night, and you take the information and use it for your own means—"

"Deidre—"

"Get away from me, Nick," she seethed, throwing off his hold and shoving her key in the lock. He grasped both of her shoulders at once in an iron-strong hold. She felt the pressure of his body against hers from behind.

"I didn't mean to upset you or betray a confidence," he breathed out quietly from just above her left ear. She went still, shivering uncontrollably at the sensation of his chin brushing her hair as he spoke. "The fact of the matter is, the truth is going to come out as soon as you receive those test results. You weren't planning on keeping the results secret, were you?"

"No, of course not." Her voice vibrated with anger, but she didn't move away from him.

"This is crucial information to me, as well as John Kellerman."

Deidre turned the key and plunged into the warm kitchen. She immediately headed toward the living room, sensing that Nick was behind her and wanting to escape. How could she have spilled her guts out to him last night? The only thing he cared about was that damn company and all the power and money that went with it. Lincoln meant so much more to her than that.

He caught her and spun her around in his arms so quickly all her breath rushed out of her lungs.

"You share control of DuBois Enterprises with me until any information comes to light that refutes that claim, Deidre." He shook her gently, a look of profound frustration tightening his features. "You can't claim to be Lincoln's daughter and then insist there are no consequences to that claim. *Of course* I'm going to communicate certain essentials about your stance on being named as one of Lincoln's heirs to John Kellerman."

"I heard what you said," she said, horrified to feel tears spill down her cheek. "The only thing you care about is my cooperation. Your being here in Harbor Town, the Christmas tree, the photos, last night…*all* of it is just your way of getting what you want out of me. You're using me."

"*No.* Didn't I tell you what happened between us last night has got absolutely nothing to do with DuBois Enterprises?" he grated out. He clamped his eyelids shut briefly and then focused on her again. "Damn it, Deidre, don't you have the smallest inkling of the repercussions of Lincoln giving you half of the controlling interest of his company?"

Doubt swamped her as she sensed the depth of his frustration, but she gave him a halfhearted glance of defiance. "I've told you I don't care about DuBois Enterprises or Lincoln's money. I just…wanted…a father."

His grasp on her upper arms tightened. He brought her closer to him, until she felt anchored by his stare. His fierce, gray eyes seemed to be the only thing keeping her from succumbing to a wave of dizziness. "Sometimes we don't get precisely what we want, Deidre."

"You think I don't know that?" she cried.

"Sometimes we get less than we bargained for," he continued as if she hadn't spoken. He leaned down over her until their stares and their mouths were aligned just inches apart. "Sometimes we get *more*. That's what you got. More. Do you have any idea how many people DuBois Enterprises employs?"

She blinked at his unexpected, harsh question.

"No," she whispered.

"Over sixty thousand employees across the world. Every single one of those people has family members who depend on them. DuBois itself is the customer for hundreds of other companies that also employ thousands of people. So while it's real simple for you to brush off DuBois Enterprises as irrelevant, it's not so easy for me and the hundreds of thousands of people that depend on it every single day of their lives to do the same."

His voice rang in her ears. She just stared at his rigid face, speechless.

"I'm sorry if you thought I broke a confidence by telling John Kellerman you'd already had the genetic testing. I'm sorry that it wasn't clear to you that I was previously Linc's sole heir," he said hoarsely. He leaned down until his forehead touched hers. Deidre's breath burned in her lungs at the contact of his skin against hers. "I'm *not* trying to take advantage of you. It's just that the circumstances here are a lot bigger than you or me."

A silence stretched. She couldn't seem to inhale a full breath.

"I'm sorry," she said, the perception of her selfishness breaking through her emotional chaos like a hot knife. It only added to her distress. "I...I hadn't been thinking of it in that way. To me, this whole situation with Lincoln is—"

"Intensely personal," he muttered, his breath brushing against her cheek. He'd sounded so grim, it shocked her when he pressed his lips against the corner of her mouth. She shuddered with emotion and a wave of physical weakness. "I understand that, too. Better than I had in the beginning. Every time you told me you could care less about DuBois Enterprises, that you only wanted to know your biological father before he left this world, you meant it literally. I get that now. But that doesn't take away from the fact that there's a much bigger, wider picture here, Deidre."

Tears coursed down her cheek. The edges of her vision were darkening. "I wish Lincoln had never changed that damn will," she mumbled through leaden lips.

His arms encircled her and he brought her hard against him. When he squeezed her tight, more unwanted tears spilled out of her eyes. He opened his hand at the base of her spine, and she had the disorienting thought he knew she had a tattoo there, although that wasn't possible—was it? Her vision swam before her eyes. His caress struck her as focused...cherishing...possessive. He spoke next to her ear, the sensation of his warm breath on her skin and the sound of his roughened voice increasing her uncontrollable trembling.

"What's done is done. We'll deal with the consequences. I just want you to know that I'm not your enemy. Please believe that. If you're truly Linc's biological daughter, if Lincoln wanted you to have partial control of his company and if he was of sound mind when he made that decision, then I will make *sure* that legacy is passed on to you. I would fight anyone tooth and nail who challenged your claim if all those things are true, *including* John Kellerman. So there's no reason to feel threatened by me telling Kellerman about the genetic testing or that you've expressed interest in the Vivicor acquisition." He leaned back and stared down into her face. She blinked the tears out of her eyes so she could see him better, but he remained blurry. Deidre had the vague impression that he looked alarmed, but she couldn't understand why.

"Deidre? *Deidre*—"

Her knees gave way. He uttered a curse as she collapsed and he caught her in his arms.

Nick watched her face anxiously as he carried Deidre down the hallway. Her eyelids fluttered, but she remained conscious. He'd nearly had a heart attack when he felt her legs give and she'd slumped in his arms. She was sick—weak—and he'd been barking at her like a rabid dog. He realized how upset she was at what she'd perceived to be a betrayal on his part. Nick had been wound up, as well. He'd been so caught up in trying to get her to understand his point of view that he'd remained utterly insensitive to the fact that she was about to faint.

He lowered her to the edge of the bed. She placed one hand on his shoulder and straightened into a sitting position.

"Lie down. I'm going to call a doctor."

"No," she said, sounding fatigued but firm. "It's just low blood sugar. I haven't been eating much over the past few days. And I'm a little tired." Something about the defiant, if weary, tilt of her chin instinctively told him she wasn't used to being the one receiving care. Deidre was usually the care-giver. She was the fighter. This couldn't be easy for her. He understood her need for independence, but she'd better get used to some help, in the short term, anyway.

"I'll be right back."

He returned a moment later with a large glass of milk and a box of granola bars. "I called your sister at the Family Center. I figured she should know you weren't feeling well. She says she's coming by, but I told her you'd be resting. Eat a couple of these to get some fuel into you," he directed, un-wrapping a bar for her.

She seemed too tired to argue. Her petite frame slumped at the edge of the bed. She ate the food he gave her mechan-ically, swallowing it down with several gulps of milk. She shook her head weakly when he handed her the last of the second granola bar.

"Why don't you lie down? Do you want some tea?"

She shook her head and managed a weak smile. "You're a regular Florence Nightingale." Some color was returning to her cheeks.

In fact, *too* much color.

"Are you all right?" he asked, noticing the light sheen of sweat on her forehead.

She nodded. "I'm hot," she whispered. "It's one of the

symptoms of low blood sugar. It'll pass in a minute, now that I've eaten."

He matter-of-factly reached for the bottom of her sweater and drew it over her head. She looked a little stunned when he tossed the garment on the end of the bed, but apparently the cool air on her skin felt too good—or she was too exhausted—to protest. He knelt and removed her leather boots, forcing his gaze to remain on his task. A few seconds later, he stood and lifted the sheets, easing her limp form beneath them. Her eyelids grew heavy the second her cheek hit the pillow.

"You need a nice, long nap," he said, tucking the sheet around her shoulders and drawing the comforter to her waist. "I knew you'd hardly been eating while you were at The Pines, but I had no idea you'd been wearing yourself out like this. I should have guessed. The staff told me you hardly left Linc's side in the days before he died."

"It was where I wanted to be," she whispered. Her gaze flickered up to meet his. He abruptly stilled. She, too, looked frozen, unable to glance away. Staring down into Deidre's eyes could make a man feel like he was sinking…falling. The seconds stretched. He felt his body sway slightly, as though he were being drawn to her like a magnet.

"Go to sleep, Deidre," he said gruffly.

She rolled on her side, her back to him. He stood next to the bed, watching her long after her breath became even and peaceful.

He walked out of the room, shutting the door behind him carefully. One hand remained on the knob. He stretched his arm and palmed the frame above the door. He leaned there, unmoving.

"Nick?"

He blinked. Colleen Kavanaugh and a tall, dark man stood

in the hallway. How long had he been leaning there, lost in thought? He hadn't even heard them enter the cottage.

"She ate a couple granola bars and drank some milk. She's sleeping soundly," he said, straightening.

"Are *you* all right?" Colleen asked him, a strange look on her face.

"Yeah. Of course," Nick replied. He walked past the concerned-looking couple to the kitchen. He didn't want their voices to wake Deidre. He automatically shook Eric Reyes's hand when Colleen introduced them.

He wondered what Colleen had witnessed on his face as he stood there at Deidre's door. She couldn't possibly know he'd been reliving the moment when he'd whisked Deidre's sweater over her head, exposing inches and inches of flawless, smooth skin and graceful, sloping shoulders. The vision of her naked, lithesome arms had made him want to do something crazy. The bra she'd worn beneath the simple sweater had surprised him a little, it was so feminine and pretty. Deidre was the epitome of feminine and pretty, granted, but she was so no-nonsense, he'd have pegged her for being the practical-lingerie type.

Instead, black lace had encased small, thrusting, firm breasts. When Colleen had called out to him, he'd been fantasizing what it'd feel like to run his mouth along the edge of that lace and feel the warm, sweet swell of flesh against his lips.

He shook his head as if to clear it.

"You're a doctor?" Nick asked Eric, who nodded.

"Do you think Deidre should go to the hospital?"

"From what I understand from Colleen and her brothers, Deidre is typically a strong woman. She's probably just dehydrated and run-down. We'll get some fluids and food into her when she wakes up. You know what stress and grief can do to a person. If I suspect it's anything more serious—"

"You'll call me," Nick said. He dug in his jeans pocket for his wallet. "Do me a favor and call me either way. I'd like to know how she's doing. Here's my number." Colleen looked taken aback but accepted his card.

"I'm sure it's just exhaustion," Colleen said, "but I'll keep you updated."

"Thanks," Nick said before he headed for the door.

He wasn't sure what exactly had hit him as he'd stared down at Deidre as she lay on that bed, but he knew one thing for sure: he wanted her too much to control it, regardless of the strange circumstances…no matter the possible consequences.

Deidre awoke three and a half hours later to the smell of chicken broth. She sat up, feeling disoriented when she noticed she was just wearing her bra and pants. The vision of Nick's fierce stare as he'd looked down as she lay in the bed flashed across her mind's eye in vivid detail.

Other memories stampeded across her brain. Nick talking so coolly on the phone about her to John Kellerman. *As for the rest, I'm not certain right now,* she remembered him saying. She'd been moved deeply by Nick's desperate entreaty to understand his position, but it hurt to know firsthand he still had his doubts about her.

She clamped her eyes shut in regret as she recalled the rest of their charged encounter. She'd *fainted.* Well, almost fainted anyway. She'd never fainted in her life. And Nick had taken her to bed and partially undressed her.

Once again, she thought of the way he'd looked when he'd stared down at her, his desire naked and exposed, a clear reflection of what must have been in her own eyes.

She placed her hand over her heart when it gave a strange throb.

After a moment, she sighed and drew on her sweater. She ran a comb through her hair and exited the bedroom.

"Are you all right?" Colleen asked anxiously when she walked into the kitchen. Her sister was standing at the stove, stirring the contents of a pot. Eric lowered the newspaper he'd been reading as he sat in the breakfast nook.

"I'm fine," Deidre said, embarrassed. "I'm sorry to have interrupted your day. You haven't been here the whole time I slept, have you?"

Colleen waved her hand dismissively and reached for a bowl. "Never mind that. How are you feeling?"

"Still dizzy?" Eric asked, standing and coming toward her.

Deidre shook her head, pausing when Eric reached to touch her brow. "I haven't got a fever," she said, embarrassed. "I feel fine now. It was my blood sugar. I didn't have an appetite this morning."

"I'll willing to bet you haven't had an appetite for weeks. Stress," Eric mumbled as he stared at the clock on the wall while he took her pulse.

"This has all been too much for you. And you haven't been sleeping well," Colleen fretted as she ladled some soup into a bowl. "Sit down and eat this."

"Yes, Mother," Deidre teased with a smile. When Eric finished taking her pulse, however, she went and ate her soup like a perfect patient. She hated being perceived as weak. Seeing the concerned expression on Colleen's face was enough to make her mend her ways and take better care of herself.

"I'm good as new," she declared as she pushed back her empty bowl. She'd wolfed down two and a half helpings, much to her shock. Colleen's cooking always had that effect on her, just like her mother's used to when she was a girl.

"The soup was delicious, thank you."

"You still need to take it easy and get plenty of rest," Eric said. "You know as well as I do the way people can run themselves down after the death of a family member."

"I might have slacked off a little bit on taking care of myself in the past few months, but I promise I'll get strict again," Deidre said quickly when she saw Colleen's brow furrow. "I've been so preoccupied with Lincoln. It all caught up with me this afternoon, I guess," she admitted as she watched Eric walk up behind the back of Colleen's chair and stroke her sister's shoulders. She grinned, happiness surging through her at the sight of Eric and Colleen's tangible love for one another.

"Now that you two made up at the rehearsal dinner, I can see I'm going to have trouble prying you apart, aren't I?" she asked the couple.

"That's the plan," Eric murmured silkily before he leaned down and gave Colleen a kiss. Deidre had liked Eric from the moment she'd met him a few nights ago. He was handsome, yes, but also aware of other people's feelings and at the top of the bell curve of intelligence. She'd known enough doctors and surgeons over the years to judge that with confidence. The main reason she liked Eric, however, was that the man was clearly crazy for Colleen.

She cleared her throat as she toyed with her soupspoon. Eric and Colleen broke apart. "Did…did Nick leave after I fell asleep?" she asked, trying to sound casual.

Colleen nodded, suddenly serious.

"He's a real puzzle, isn't he?" Eric asked. "I got the impression from Colleen he was suspicious of you and this business of Lincoln DuBois's will, but he was acting like he'd take on a whole platoon single-handed to ensure your safety when we got here this afternoon."

"Nick was standing at your bedroom door like a watchdog when we arrived," Colleen informed her quietly. "He looked so intense, I wondered if his stare could burn a hole through the door."

Deidre's cheeks turned hot. She knew precisely what Colleen meant about Nick's stare.

"He's an enigma, all right," she said before she changed the subject.

Deidre had to promise Eric and Colleen at least half a dozen times she'd take it easy that night and get plenty of rest. The couple left at nightfall to go and pick up Coleen's children, Brendan and Jenny, from Brigit's house. Deidre took a long, hot bath once she was alone. At around five o'clock that afternoon, her cell phone began to ring. She tensed, dread welling up inside her. The response had been programmed into her since coming to Harbor Town. She'd been worried about her mother calling. Increasingly, she was also growing anxious about receiving the call about the genetic testing from GenLabs. She told herself she was being ridiculous. Surely it'd be a week or more before she received that call.

She checked the number and saw an unfamiliar prefix. She answered, her heart starting to race.

"Hello?"

"Am I forgiven?"

A rush of warmth went through her when she recognized Nick's blunt, matter-of-fact voice.

"I suppose, seeing as you did your part to revive me," she said, smiling.

"How are you feeling?"

"Embarrassed, mostly. That's never happened to me before."

"I kind of figured. You didn't seem too happy about it. I guess it's true what they say about doctors and nurses making the worst patients."

She wandered over to the pretty Christmas tree and ran her fingers over some soft needles. "I was very compliant when Colleen fed me. I'm much better, I promise."

"It's amazing how the body needs little things like food

and sleep," he murmured mildly enough. Maybe it was her guilt that made her hear a hint of remonstrance.

"I'll take care of myself. I honestly hadn't noticed how run-down I'd gotten."

"Neither had I. I knew you hadn't had much of an appetite while you were at The Pines, but I'm kicking myself for not realizing how bad things had gotten."

Deidre swallowed thickly. It wasn't his job to monitor her physical health, after all. She couldn't help but recall how Colleen had said Nick had been standing at her door like a watchdog.

A charged silence ensued.

"I'm sorry about shouting at you the way I did," he said.

"You didn't shout at me. What you said was true. I need to come out of my shell and look at the bigger picture here. There are a lot of people depending on DuBois Enterprises. Lincoln would have wanted me to understand that."

Was that relief she heard in his ragged sigh?

"I'm going to give you the number for Abel Warren—Lincoln's personal attorney. He's handling the will. He'll be able to explain the details of the will and give you the information for how to access your funds. He'll probably want to fly out here to see you."

"No," Deidre said quickly. "I'm not ready for that yet. I'd rather wait for the genetic testing before I make any moves in that direction."

"If that's what you want, but I still want you to have Abel's number. He can inform you of your legal rights, Deidre. I'll text his number to you, and you'll have it for reference."

Deidre couldn't find a reason to disagree with that. It was hard to explain to Nick that it was daunting to try to plan a life that was precariously perched on shifting sands, especially since he seemed like one of the aspects that might change at any moment.

"Do you think you'll feel up to going out tomorrow afternoon?" he asked.

"I feel up to going out now, to be honest." She smiled when she heard his doubtful grunt. "Don't worry. I promised to rest up tonight. What did you have in mind for tomorrow afternoon? Do we need to discuss something else about DuBois?"

"I'd like to get your signature for the Vivicor transaction, if you're still agreeable. More importantly, I just want to take you out, if you're up for it."

Her stroking fingers paused on the Christmas tree. "To do what?"

"It's a surprise. I hope you like it. Just dress warmly—we're supposed to have light snow—and be ready by two o'clock."

She agreed and said goodbye. His mysteriousness only added to her sense of excitement in regard to spending time with him. He may have been secretive about the details, but she was fairly certain about one thing.

Nick Malone had just asked her for a date.

Chapter Five

She did as she'd promised and ate and slept well that night, feeling refreshed and stronger when she awoke. The morning was spent doing some light exercises and stretches, relaxing and reading. She was finishing brushing her teeth when she heard a car door slam.

She grabbed her coat, a scarf and some gloves when she reached the kitchen, slamming the door behind her as Nick paused in his ascent of the front steps. A red, black and white flannel shirt peeked from beneath his black insulated jacket. His hair was tousled and whiskers shadowed his jaw. He looked windblown and outdoorsy…and sexy as hell.

"Hi," she said, suddenly feeling ridiculously shy when she looked into his gray eyes. The kiss they'd shared the other night had been smoking hot, but somehow, their stormy encounter yesterday had been more…intimate.

"Hi," he returned, a small smile shaping his mouth.

Yes, something had definitely happened yesterday, Deidre

confirmed when she saw his eyes move over her warmly. It was as if both of them had silently admitted that while there may be potential stress and unresolved conflict between them, there was also attraction—and plenty of it.

"Are you ready to go?"

She nodded, taking the hand he offered when she approached him. She gave him a smile and before she could take the first step on the stairs, he leaned down. A shiver of delight went through her when he touched his mouth to hers. He must have spent some time outdoors before he got in his car, because his lips were firm and cool. He'd meant it as a kiss of greeting, Deidre suspected, but it felt so good to be genuine in her attraction toward him. She put her arms around his shoulders and kissed him back, warming his lips with her own. It felt wonderful to give herself permission to kiss him. He smelled like spice and fresh air. He tasted like he'd just eaten something sweet.

"That was nice," she said quietly next to his lips when she sealed their kiss.

His gray eyes flashed.

"I'll say it is," he muttered, and suddenly he was the one kissing her. He took her into his arms and lifted her against his body, until her boots left the porch. While Deidre's kiss had been airy and teasing, Nick's was demanding and consuming. She let go—surrendered to the sensation of him for an untold period of time. She blinked open her eyes when the pressure of his mouth left hers a while later and his lips brushed her nose.

"I'm not sure I can control what might happen if you start to be nice to me," he said quietly, his warm breath causing vapor to billow between them.

She leaned back an inch and examined him with mock seriousness. "Would you rather I stopped?"

"Don't you dare," he growled softly.

She smiled and kissed him again. He groaned, seizing her mouth in a quick, voracious kiss before he set her boots back on the stairs. "Come on, or your surprise will get cold."

"My surprise?" she asked, as she followed him down the steps, her hand in his. "What is it?"

But Nick refused to give a word of explanation concerning the enigmatic surprise when they got into his sedan, and he drove several miles through the white and gray, barren country landscape.

"McGraw Stables?" Deidre asked in confusion when he turned down a wooded lane and she saw a large red, gold and brown sign featuring a large barn and several galloping horses. As they got closer to several buildings in the distance, she noticed the trees lining the lane were decorated with white Christmas lights. "But I told you when we were at Lincoln's that I don't ride," she explained. Both Nick and Lincoln were horse aficionados. Lincoln reportedly owned one of the finest horse stables in all of Nevada and California.

"I know. You won't have to ride for this," Nick assured her as he pulled his sedan into a turnabout before a long, low building and parked. To the left, Deidre saw an attractive white farmhouse. Her attention was diverted, however, by the sound of jingling bells.

"Oh, how pretty," she said breathlessly. A man led a horse with a sleek brown coat toward them. The horse was hooked up to a wooden wagon decorated for the Christmas season with evergreen garland and tinkling bells. The man paused fifteen feet or so away from Nick's car. The horse tossed her head and stomped her front feet in an impatient gesture.

"We better get going. Maybelle doesn't like to wait, apparently," Nick murmured.

"Maybelle? Is that her name?" Deidre asked a moment later when they'd alighted from the car. Snow flurries pelted her cheeks as she approached the prancing horse. "Hey there,

Maybelle. You're a beauty," Deidre crooned when the mare turned her head and looked at her with liquid brown eyes. She glanced over and met the stare of the man holding Maybelle's bridle. He had a bland, unremarkable face, but his hazel eyes were warm when he looked at her.

"Hi," Deidre said.

He nodded at her in greeting. "She's all ready for you. Addy put a thermos of hot chocolate under the seat, along with some of those sugar cookies you liked this morning, Nick."

Nick laughed as he helped Deidre up the wooden steps of the wagon. "If I rode at your stables regularly, Addy would put twenty pounds on me in a month or two. Addy and Evan own the McGraw Stables," Nick explained to Deidre, nodding toward the man before he clambered up the steps after Deidre.

"It's a perfect day for this," Evan said, stepping back when Nick took the reins and sat next to Deidre. "Hardly a breeze. You're free to use any of the paths on our property that you've ridden before, and the old lake road, as well. Everything's been plowed pretty recently," Evan explained. "When you get back, Addy will have an early dinner ready for you." He winked at Deidre. "It's all part of the carriage rental package."

Nick gave her an amused glance as he reached beneath the wagon seat and withdrew a hefty mug. He handed it to her and then reached for a thermos. "Addy is an excellent cook. We'd be fools to turn down the offer for dinner."

Deidre laughed as Nick wedged the thermos between his thighs and unscrewed it. "Well, I'm no fool. It sounds wonderful," she told Evan. Evan nodded and gave them a wave before he returned to the stables.

"How in the world did you find out about this place?" she asked as the delicious aroma of sweet chocolate wafted up to her nose.

He shrugged slightly and poured some of the steaming liquid into her cup. "I didn't think it'd hurt to ask around about local stables since I was planning to be in Harbor Town for a while."

"And you couldn't imagine being anywhere without being able to ride for a period of time, could you?" she said, understanding hitting her. He'd ridden every day when he'd been at The Pines. She took a sip of the hot chocolate.

"Oh, yum."

"Wait till you try this," he said, replacing the thermos. He poked his hand under the seat and withdrew a baking tin from beneath the seat. She took it and opened the lid.

"Ooh," she murmured, ginning as she picked up a perfect, delectable-looking iced Christmas tree cookie from the tin.

"They're really good. I had a couple this morning when I came out to arrange the carriage rental."

Deidre bit into the cookie. It melted on her tongue, tasting like fresh butter, sugar and Christmastime itself. She grinned happily and met his stare. "*These* are why you tasted so sweet," she murmured as she chewed the cookie, referring to their earlier kiss.

He swept down and covered her mouth with his, pausing to slide his tongue along the seam of her lips. She went completely still next to him. He lifted his head. His gray eyes smoldered.

"Just wanted to experience the same thing you did. You're right. Sweet," he said, a grin ghosting his lips.

It took several heartbeats before she remembered to breathe.

He retrieved several folded blankets from beneath the seat, tucking them beneath her with brisk, mechanical precision. His hand moving over her hips and thighs felt the opposite of mundane to Deidre, however. Maybe he wasn't as matter-of-fact as she'd thought, however, because his fingers lingered over the outer curve of her rear end. He looked up into her face, and Deidre felt that increasingly familiar swooping sensation in her belly.

She became entranced by the black specks in the iris of his eyes. They both blinked and glanced at the front of the sleigh when Maybelle snorted impatiently.

He released the brake and gave the reins an almost imperceptible twitch. Maybelle responded immediately, swinging the wagon in the turnabout. Deidre felt warm and content beneath the blankets, her steaming hot chocolate clutched in her gloved hand, Nick's solid frame pressing against her side.

The paths that led through the McGraws' wooded property were picturesque on the snowy winter's day. Eventually, Nick directed Maybelle onto the old lakefront road. The road wasn't used much anymore by vehicles, but it was maintained by the town for summer biking and Rollerblade use. Several inches of fresh snow lay on it, but Maybelle seemed to have no difficulty maneuvering through it, her trotting hooves tossing up snow with jaunty ease.

Nick and she conversed together comfortably, Deidre occasionally pointing out landmarks at the outskirts of town and asking Nick questions about horses.

"I'll teach you how to ride, if you like," he said as they rattled along and the bells attached to the garland jingled merrily.

"I don't know. I'd probably make a fool of myself."

"You won't," he said, so confidently she glanced at him in amazement. He gave her a sidelong glance. "You're an athlete, aren't you? And I've seen how horses respond to you. Remember when I came upon you when we were at The Pines stables and you were talking to that stallion? Horses are in your blood."

Deidre kept her gaze on Maybelle's gleaming hindquarters. For a second, her heart had jumped at his words. Was he starting to believe she was Lincoln DuBois's daughter? With a sinking feeling, she realized a moment later he might have just been referring to her mother's skills as a horsewoman. She'd discovered from Lincoln that Brigit had been a junior championship jumper as a teenager. Brigit had never once mentioned being an accomplished equestrian the entire time Deidre was growing up.

Nick and she were having such a wonderful time, she didn't want to ruin it by asking him to clarify what he'd meant by horses being "in her blood."

She shivered minutes later when a breeze whipped past them and snow flurries batted against her exposed skin. Nick slid his arm behind her back and pulled her against his side, still holding the reins with his left hand. She cuddled against him, her cheek pressed against his jacket, mesmerized by the sound of Maybelle's trotting hooves and the feeling of Nick next to her. The lake stretched next to them like a swath of ruffled steel-blue fabric. Her nose felt cold, but her belly was warm from the hot chocolate. She couldn't recall ever feeling such a strange combination of contentment and anticipation in her life.

They paused a while later when they came to the terminus of the road. Deidre pointed out the enormous sand dunes lining the lake in the distance.

"Have you ever dune dived?" she asked Nick.

He grimaced. "At the risk of knocking myself down a few notches in your estimation, I'll admit I'm not much of a swimmer or diver."

She gave him an assessing glance. "You're an athlete. I could teach you," she teased, repeating what he'd told her about horseback riding.

He laughed under his breath. "I doubt it. Teaching a cowboy how to swim is like teaching a fish to walk." His gaze narrowed on the massive, tall dunes. "Don't tell me you actually *dived* into Lake Michigan from those things."

"Sure."

His gaze ran over her face admiringly. "That's something I'd like to see," he admitted quietly.

"We'll have to come back in July."

Something flickered across his stark features that made her mirth fade. She studied her gloved hands on top of the dark red wool blanket, silently railing at herself for her impulsive words.

"Yeah," he said before he flicked his wrist and chirruped to Maybelle and the taut moment had passed.

Mrs. Addy McGraw possessed the kind of face that was easy to like—open, weathered and nearly always smiling. Her girth was wide, but Addy appeared to be in robust health from her regular labor in the stables.

Addy met them in the turnabout near the stables when they returned late that afternoon. She wore boots, a parka and a beat-up old brown suede cowboy hat on her short gray hair. Addy directed Nick into the designated area of a large red barn, where they descended from the wagon. She started to greet Deidre, but became distracted when she noticed Nick starting to unharness Maybelle.

"Now, you're a paying guest here, you leave that to Evan and I," she scolded Nick. "You two run on inside to the kitchen. I've got some hot buttered rum on the stove for you. Evan and I will be there in a jiff, and we'll have ourselves a nice early dinner," she said, beaming at Deidre.

The kitchen of the handsome, white-shingled farmhouse was comfortably old-fashioned, with Formica countertops, a colorful tablecloth and dozens of interesting appliances that appeared to be manufactured anywhere from the 1950s to the 1970s. A divine aroma of chicken and vegetables emanated from the oven. Nick and Deidre sat at the kitchen table and sipped the delicious hot buttered rum and tried to guess at the purpose of some of the more unusual-looking appliances.

He looked so appealing to her sitting there, his hair windblown, his casual clothing perfectly fitting the farmhouse kitchen.

"I find it hard to believe you're a CEO of a huge company when you look so comfortable here."

He blinked and glanced around. "In a kitchen?"

"No," she said laughing. "In a country setting. I remember thinking the same when I used to see you on the grounds at The Pines or in Lincoln's stables."

"I do miss the country when I'm in the city. But being comfortable in the country doesn't mean you can't also be a good businessman. There's a lot in common between working with horses, for example, and being a CEO."

Deidre laughed, sure he was kidding. When he sipped his buttered rum, however, his expression entirely somber, she asked, "You're not joking? What do working with horses and being a CEO have in common?"

"Instinct. I can read people because I learned how to read animals first."

Deidre opened her mouth to reply, but paused at the sound of the back door opening and the stamping of boots on the back porch. Nick and Deidre stood from the table when Addy and Evan entered the kitchen. Nick started to introduce Addy and Deidre, as there hadn't been the opportunity when they arrived.

"You don't have to tell me who this girl is," Addy boomed, surprising Deidre by giving her a big hug. "I recognized you the moment I saw you in the wagon. You're Brigit Kavanaugh's girl, Deidre. Who else could you be, looking like you do? I've got the perfect horse in mind for you, too," she added confidentially.

Deidre laughed, feeling bewildered. "I didn't realize you knew my mother."

Addy looked taken aback. She gave Evan a meaningful glance. "*Knew* her? Brigit's daughter is standing here, saying she didn't realize we knew her mother," Addy said to Evan as if Deidre had been babbling nonsense. Nick noticed both Deidre and Addy's confusion and intervened.

"Your mother has been a regular rider at the McGraw Stables a long time, Deidre," Nick said.

Deidre looked at him, her brow crinkled. "How did you know that?"

He shrugged. "Addy and I got to talking."

"I first met your Mom twenty-eight years ago," Addy explained as she pulled a casserole from the oven. She seemed forever in motion. "Isn't that right, Evan?" she asked her husband as he sat at the table and sipped some coffee.

"That's right," Evan agreed, nodding and smiling at Deidre. "Finer horsewoman I've never witnessed. You certainly do have the look of her."

"Evan has always had a little crush on your mama," Addy told Deidre with the air of someone telling a mischievous secret. Evan muttered under his breath and blushed.

"Deidre hasn't been in Harbor Town for years now," Nick tried to explain to the McGraws. "She's been—"

"In the Middle East, and recently Germany, doing her nursing. We know all about it," Addy assured him. "Deidre, the plates and glasses are in that cabinet there, the silverware in that drawer. Would you mind?"

"Of course not. It's my pleasure," Deidre muttered, hurrying to help, her mind spinning. "I think part of the misunderstanding," she explained as she laid the silverware, "is that I never knew my mother even rode horses until recently."

Addy did a double take from where she stood at the counter ladling gravy into a bowl.

"You didn't know Brigit rode? Why wouldn't Brigit tell you about that?"

Deidre kept her gaze lowered. Thankfully, Nick noticed her discomfort.

"None of Brigit's children ride," he said. "The Kavanaugh children's athletic talents lie in other areas. Deidre, for instance, is an expert diver and water-skier."

"Well that's something," Addy complimented her, even though she still looked puzzled. She walked over to the table and set down a delectable-looking platter of baked chicken surrounded by golden-brown roasted potatoes. She removed the lid of the casserole dish and Deidre inhaled the smell of broccoli and cheese. Her stomach growled despite a topic that disturbed her, for some reason. "You all sit down now and start to dig in.

"Even if you are a swimmer and a diver, that doesn't mean you aren't a horsewoman, Deidre," Addy added a moment later as she set a basket of steaming rolls on the table and sat down.

"I keep telling her that," Nick said, his gaze on Deidre as he forked a potato onto his plate.

Addy pointed at Nick. "Well if *that* boy, who knows horses better than Evan and I combined, says you're a rider, then you're a rider!" Addy declared, as if there was no point in further discussing the topic. "There's no way you could look so much like your mama and not be a horsewoman. I still can't imagine why Brigit never brought you kids to the stables, though. I never thought about it much, but it *is* very odd, isn't it?"

Deidre stopped chewing. Nick neatly changed the subject.

"I'm sorry about Addy's questions about your mother," Nick said later as they pulled out of the McGraw Stables in Nick's car.

"There's nothing to apologize for. I had a wonderful time. How can you apologize for taking me for a ride in a horse-drawn wagon and then for the best home-cooked meal I've had in a long while? Addy could give my mother a run for her money when it comes to cooking," she said, staring out the window of the sedan into the dark night.

"She's a bit on the blunt side. I'm sorry if she made you uncomfortable," he said, giving her a sideways glance.

"It's okay," Deidre mumbled. He came to a halt at a four-way intersection. Nick's was the only vehicle within seeing distance on the desolate country road.

"Is it?"

"Yes. Of course," Deidre said, laughing. She didn't want to dwell on her mother when it'd been such a magical day so far. "I have an idea. Do you know what we should do?"

He raised his eyebrows but remained silent. Even though the interior of the car was dim, she noticed the subtle change in his expression. An electric, tingly sensation flickered in her belly. She licked her lower lip anxiously and stared out the front window, her heart starting to throb in her chest.

"Do you want to go Christmas shopping with me? I haven't gotten my family anything yet."

He began to drive again. She wondered if she'd disappointed him with her blasé suggestion, given the heat of his stare just then.

"Tell me where to go. I'm at your command," he said, his light tone reassuring her.

She had more fun than she thought she would shopping at Harbor Town's finest establishments—Dora's Fashion Station; Health and Team Athletics; and, of course, the renowned Shop and Save, where they stocked every item on her nieces' and nephew's Christmas lists.

"You're laughing at my expense," she admonished Nick

later that night as they left Health and Team Athletics. He wasn't really laughing, only smirking, which Deidre was learning was the equivalent of roaring with mirth when it came to Nick. He only shrugged as he opened the trunk and placed several bags into it.

"That manager and salesman were fawning all over you like you were a movie star returning to her hometown," he said, referring to two men in the shop who had recognized Deidre. The manager had been a few years older than her, and Chip, the salesman, a few years younger. She hadn't recognized either man, but they'd known her. Both of them had lit up on seeing her, rushing over to greet her and tell her how much they used to enjoy watching her water-skiing shows years back.

"I had no idea you were so famous," Nick mused, still wearing that small grin as they drove down Main Street through the light snow.

Deidre wasn't just embarrassed, her cheeks were hot enough to fry bacon on them. She'd had no idea her summer job during high school and college would be so well remembered in Harbor Town. She'd taken on the lead role in a Mackinaw Island water show purely out of a need for money. After she'd gone to college, she'd refused to take financial assistance from Brigit. She hadn't done a ski jump or—heaven forbid—been the apex of a skiers' triangle since she was twenty-one years old.

It embarrassed her to think of Nick considering her as some of the townspeople did—a racy female daredevil in a skimpy bathing suit.

Nick had hired someone to investigate her past, hadn't he? What sorts of photos had he seen of her, performing at water shows in tiny bikinis? It certainly might have been evidence that added fuel to his doubts about her character. He'd prob-

ably thought of her as the equivalent of a showgirl. No wonder he'd been so suspicious of her.

Had John Kellerman, DuBois's chief legal officer, also
seen those photos? Had *Lincoln?*

She blushed again in embarrassment, rising out of her
thoughts when she realized Nick had put the car in Park in
the driveway of Cedar Cottage.

He reached into the backseat and withdrew a manila envelope. "I hope this doesn't kill the mood," he muttered, looking a little regretful.

"Is it the forms you need me to sign for the Vivicor acquisition?" she asked.

"Yeah."

"It's not going to kill the mood," she said, feeling guilty
again when she recalled all the accusations she'd made yesterday about him using her to get her cooperation. She didn't
really believe that.

She didn't *want* to believe it. Not when she was so attracted to Nick.

She gave him a reassuring smile before she reached for
the car door latch. "Come on inside. I'll make some decaf
and we can look at the papers."

"You can contact Abel Warren, Lincoln's personal lawyer, and have him advise you before you sign," Nick said half
an hour later. He'd just given her an overview of the transaction. They sat on the sofa side by side, coffee cups on the
table before them. Deidre held the necessary papers in her
lap. "Abel is an impartial party. He'll advise you just as he
would have Lincoln."

She met his stare, a pen poised in her hand. "Lincoln
wouldn't have asked Abel for advice on the matter. He would
have trusted your decision. That's why he hired you to run
his company."

His mouth flattened.

"Is there some reason I need impartial legal advice?" she asked slowly. "I'm just agreeing to an acquisition that will benefit DuBois Enterprises, right?"

Nick nodded, but his mouth remained tight. He suddenly reached over and grabbed the pen and packet of papers from her. He tossed them on the table.

"Nick, what are you—"

"I don't want you to regret signing anything." He put his arms around her, and she gazed up at him in amazement.

"I won't regret it. You've served DuBois Enterprises faithfully for years. I trust you to make good business decisions," she whispered, stunned by the focused heat in his eyes.

"Business can wait," he said. "This can't."

He covered her mouth when she opened it to speak. She moaned when she came into contact with his heat. All the anticipation, all the desire that had been building in her since he'd looked down at her as she lay in bed yesterday sparked and flared high at his kiss.

His mouth felt hot and persuasive moving over hers. He altered the angle of his head and penetrated her lips with his tongue, his hunger a palpable thing. She melted beneath his bold claim, stroking him back eagerly, sliding her tongue against his, thrilling at the tension that sprung into his muscles. His kiss was so addictive that she made a muffled sound of protest when he ended it.

"I want you. A lot. I know I'm just stating the obvious," he said next to her mouth, the sound of his ragged male desire sending a prickle of excitement through her.

"I want you, too," she admitted, letting her lips slide against his, caressing, kissing, nibbling. "But maybe it's a bad idea for us to give in to it? We'll probably regret it."

"How in the hell could I ever regret having you?"

Something jumped in her stomach at the sound of his disbelief mingling with stark desire. Nevertheless, she grasped at rational thought, trying to gird herself against his appeal.

"What if you ended up taking me to court?" she whispered, meeting his stare. "You don't think it would be problematic that we'd previously slept together? Not exactly neat and clean."

"This whole thing has been messy from the start. Maybe we ought to embrace that fact instead of run from it."

She stared into his face, looking for some sign of what was the right thing to do in this situation. She saw nothing but a virile, attractive man who clearly desired her.

He leaned close. "I want you to understand something, Deidre. If it should ever come to any kind of legal action in regard to Lincoln's will, it would have nothing to do with you personally and everything to do with the well-being of DuBois Enterprises. Are you certain you don't want to learn the business?" he asked her intently.

"Yes. I can't even imagine it, Nick."

"That's not certainty. That's ignorance of the task at hand. You're intelligent. You could learn. I could teach you."

"Do I have to decide right this second? Shouldn't we establish without a doubt whether or not I am Lincoln's daughter?"

He leaned back, staring at the Christmas tree with his brow furrowed.

"What?" she queried.

"I promised myself I wasn't going to talk to you about the will today."

Deidre chuckled. "It just goes to show you how money and power has a way of intruding into any situation."

He met her gaze. Her smile faded when she registered his expression.

"I don't accept that," he said before he leaned over and captured her mouth again in a blistering kiss. She whimpered as his consumption continued. Their mouths fused, tongues and lips moving together in a warm, liquid friction. Her hand found its way to his collar where she delved her fingers through his thick hair. She loved the feeling of it so much, she let her other hand join in the pleasure. He groaned, low and rough, when she scraped his scalp with her fingernails. Deidre grasped his head, holding on for dear life as desire coiled tight inside of her. Nick's words—and her own internal conflict—warred in the background of her increasing arousal.

This whole thing has been messy from the start. Maybe we ought to embrace that fact instead of run from it.

If it should ever come to any kind of legal action, it would have nothing to do with you personally.

She thought of all the bonds of love and friendship that had been torn asunder when the Itani and Reyes families had taken Brigit to court following the accident Derry had caused. Deidre had left Harbor Town by that time, but Marc had conveyed the brutal, heart-wrenching details to her. Courtrooms could become emotional battlefields.

She moaned, miserable at the idea of breaking contact with Nick. She did it anyway.

"What?" he asked, his voice rough and sexy.

"I don't know what the right thing to do is," she whispered.

She hated how his gaze became shuttered. Desire didn't soften Nick, necessarily—in fact, his body and focus seemed to tighten beyond their typical readiness for action. What desire did to Nick was open him, invite her to enter and relish the pleasure of an attractive, complex man. Seeing him start to withdraw from her again, even slightly, hurt more than she'd expected.

She felt her grip on rationality slipping. He leaned down so that their faces were only inches apart. She inhaled the smell of soap and subtle, spicy cologne and felt her body respond.

"There's not going to be a shooting star to tell you whether it's right or wrong," he said. "You have to trust me in this, Deidre."

She swallowed thickly. Doubts assailed her, but his male scent dulled them. Her lips still felt tender and hot from his kisses, as if the nerve endings had been awakened and clamored for more pressure…more pleasure.

"You're the chief executive officer of DuBois Enterprises. You can't tell me you wouldn't regret it tomorrow."

"I'm a man, not a job. Like I said, there's no way in hell I'll *ever* regret making love to you."

It was like standing on the edge of a cliff. Maybe she should have demurred, but her heart pounded with excitement.

And she was a diver, after all.

She gave a breathless consent.

Chapter Six

He moved so rapidly, so surely, Deidre realized he must have been waiting on a precipice of anticipation, as well. He stood, swept her into his arms and headed for the hallway. He ate up the space with a long-legged stride and kicked the door to the master suite open wide. Deidre smiled and laid her cheek next to his chest. His hastiness in the matter pleased her.

He set her on the edge of the bed. The light from the hallway spilled into the darkened room, letting her see his shadowed face. She waited, her heart starting to perform a drumroll on her breastbone.

He reached out and touched her cheek.

"Thank you for trusting me," he said, his fingertips running over her jaw and neck, making her shiver.

"I could say the same of you," she whispered.

For a few seconds, he stroked her and the silence seemed to press on her eardrums.

"You have the face of a rebel angel. You're the most beautiful woman I've ever laid eyes on."

"Thank you," she mouthed soundlessly, stirred to her core by the rough gentleness of his voice.

He came down over her, easing her onto the mattress. His mouth settled on hers. She loved the feel of his weight on her. He was so hot…so hard. She drank in his elemental maleness, never before feeling the stark power of her own soft femininity than at the moment, because of the delicious contrast of their straining bodies.

He lifted his head, his hands encircling her waist. He moved, sliding her along the comforter with him until they lay on their sides facing each other, their heads resting on the pillows. His mouth continued to coax her, enliven her as it moved over her lips, cheek and neck, demanding and feverish.

She slid her fingers just beneath his shirt and rubbed. The sensation of his smooth, thick skin covering dense, warm muscle made her grasp both sides of his shirt and part them. The sounds of the snaps popping sent a thrill of excitement through her. She broke their kiss and pressed her face between the cloth, loving the taste of his naked skin, the texture of the springy hair on his chest. He made a low, rough, desperate sound.

He opened both of his hands on her waist, the gesture a blatant reminder of how much larger he was than her, how much of her he could hold in his grasp. She pressed feverish kisses over his chest. He slid his hands upward along the fabric of her sweater, plumping her breasts from below with the hard ridge of his forefinger and thumb. She responded to the erotic caress by tasting a small, erect nipple with her tongue. He made a muffled sound in his throat and covered her breasts with his hands.

She whimpered against his skin while he molded her to his palms.

"Nick," she pleaded softly.

"I know. I'm going to undress you." She helped him by raising her arms when he drew her sweater over her head. She shivered uncontrollably when he opened his hand at her waist and slid it over her belly.

"As soft as I thought you'd be. Softer." He held her stare as his long fingers slipped beneath the waistband of her jeans and he deftly unbuttoned the fly. The movement of his hand next to her stomach and pelvis caused a molten sensation to spread at her core. "Turn over on your belly."

"Wha—" she asked, confused by his request.

"It's okay," he assured. He put his hand on her shoulder and guided her. She'd never felt so vulnerable—or so excited—as she lay there on her stomach and he began to slide her jeans down over her hips. She gasped in aroused surprise when he leaned down and pressed his mouth to the base of her spine.

"I've wanted to do that ever since I saw it," he grated out roughly as he kissed her tattoo; shivers of pleasure rippled up her spine.

He pressed his hot mouth just above the crevice of her buttocks, and Deidre knew he kissed the base of her brilliant rose tattoo that included a golden caduceus spiraling up the stem. She'd gotten the tattoo in an impulsive moment a year ago in Germany. Until that second, it had been a private, secret indulgence. Or so she'd thought.

"When…when did you see my tattoo?" she asked in a strangled voice.

"I went into the workout facility at The Pines one afternoon a few months back and you were on the treadmill with your back to me. I saw it then—most of it anyway. I've been waiting to see the rest." One of his hands cradled her hip as he continued to study her tattoo with his lips and tongue. She shivered in rising excitement. "You don't wear much when you work out, Deidre."

"I didn't know I'd have an audience."

"An avid one."

She muffled a moan by pressing her mouth against the pillow when he slipped his hand beneath the satin of her panties and shaped one of her bottom cheeks to his palm. She'd never felt herself to be the focus of so much desire in her life. His mouth rose along her spine, kissing, licking, biting gently at the sensitive skin on either side of the vertebrae. When he reached the cloth of her bra, he flicked open the fastener so effortlessly, she blinked. Then his mouth was back on her skin, finding her neck while his hand explored the contours of her thighs and hip.

"Give me your mouth," he muttered, and she twisted her torso. His lips found hers, his tongue a sleek, demanding invader. Again, she drowned in his taste, turning on her hip and drawing closer, seeking more…needing more. Her entire body was going liquid with desire. She felt his hand slide along her thigh and realized dazedly he was drawing her jeans off her legs. He broke their kiss and leaned down to peel off her socks. Her breath caught when he caressed her calf and lingered on her thigh. She panted softly when he lay down next to her. He raised a hand and slowly removed her bra, baring her to his gaze.

"Look at you," he murmured quietly. Enough light flooded in from the hallway that she was able to watch his face as he examined her. He looked transfixed, his expression almost grim with desire. She shivered when his hand coasted along the side of her waist and ribs and then lingered on a breast. His hand covered her. Her nipples tightened almost painfully. He gave a low groan before he seized her mouth again. She fumbled with his shirt, baring his torso and touching him greedily. He finessed her sensitive nipple with his fingertips.

Desire sluiced through her, so sharp she broke their kiss and gave a plaintive cry.

His exploring hand lowered, stroking her hips and belly. He murmured broken words of praise into her ear—a ragged, passionate anthem. Deidre felt herself melting into a heady sensual torpor, utterly intoxicated by the sound of Nick's rough voice and the sensation of his talented, stroking hand.

He slid beneath her panties.

His fingers sought. She parted her thighs for him, wanting to be found.

His groan sounded like it scorched his throat.

She heard his voice as if from a distance as she drowned in sensation. His fingertips may be blunt and large, but he knew precisely what to do with them. He kissed her mouth more slowly than before, deliberately, languorously. He watched her face through heavy, narrowed eyelids. A delicious burn grew in her until she moaned in mounting excitement and bit at his lower lip, taunting him into giving her what she needed.

"That's right," he growled. "*That's* the Deidre I know."

He bent his head and covered the tip of her breast with his warm, wet mouth, laving a nipple with his tongue. When he drew on her firmly, she cried out.

She grasped for his waist as pleasure broke in her flesh, her fingers sinking beneath his leather belt and scraping warm skin as if she thought the wave of sensation would drown her. He pressed his finger into her body as she climaxed. She shuddered around him.

"I think you might have been meant for my touch."

Had Nick really muttered that? As Deidre lay there shaking, helpless in the clutch of desire, she had a sneaking suspicion that even if it had been her imagination, it'd been the truth.

* * *

He looped his arm beneath her as she shuddered, wanting to absorb every shiver of pleasure racking her body. He brought her against his chest, his hand still between her thighs. His jaw clenched tight at the sensation of her small breasts pressing against his chest, her nipples hard with arousal. Her skin was exquisitely soft. He hadn't been lying when he'd whispered he'd never felt anything like it. He experienced an overwhelming desire to feel every square inch of it sliding against his own skin, against his fingertips, his lips…his tongue.

Her tremors of release eased. She was small, feminine and soft, yet her muscles felt sleek and strong beneath his touch. Her curves fit his hand like she'd been built to specification.

She parted her lips, panting. He plucked at her mouth with his own, his hunger swelling at the sight of Deidre's face dewy with release. He stroked her skin while she calmed, soothing her until he couldn't take the ache of his desire a second longer.

He whipped his shirt over his shoulders and attacked the belt on his jeans. She murmured something unintelligible and started to help him, her fingers twining with his as he unfastened his fly. He hissed when her fingers brushed against the hard ridge of his arousal.

She glanced up at him, her eyes looking enormous in her flushed face. She held his gaze while she traced his contour through his clothing.

It was too much for him. He could endure a lot. He *had* endured a lot, keeping himself on a straining leash when it came to his attraction to her. But witnessing renewed desire replace satiation on Deidre's face while her fingers learned his shape shattered his restraint completely.

He muttered a curse under his breath and shed his remaining clothing like it'd caught fire. He hurriedly located a condom in his wallet.

She opened her arms to him when he came down over her. He groaned at the feeling of her warm, silky skin pressing against his. Entering Deidre was torture and bliss blended. He took her mouth in a kiss, glorying in how she sensed his need, rose to it and matched his passion.

"You're so small," he whispered next to her mouth in a choked voice a few seconds later. "I don't want to hurt you."

"You're not going to hurt me, Nick."

Her hands glided across his hips, giving him her assurance…

…her blessing.

He applied pressure and closed his eyes, begging for the strength to endure the agonizing sweetness of the moment. Sweat beaded his brow. Her body's embrace was tight and warm and every bit as perfect as the rest of her.

Nick had a fleeting thought before he was swept away by torrential pleasure. Fusing his flesh to Deidre's felt like returning to a home he never knew he'd had.

Later, they lay with their limbs entwined. Deidre felt sublimely surrounded by Nick. The scent of him filled her nose. Their pounding hearts pressed close, slowing in tandem. Her eyelids grew heavy as he stroked her hair.

"Are you asleep?" he asked after a while.

"No," she whispered. She burrowed her face between his neck and shoulder and kissed him, smiling to herself when his hold on her tightened. "I think you might have been right."

"About what?"

She lifted her head and lay it on the pillow next to his, meeting his stare. "It is sort of hard to regret something like that."

She pressed her lips against the ghost of a smile on his

mouth. "Not hard. Impossible," he said, before their mouths fused in a melting kiss.

"Can I ask you about a sensitive topic?" he asked her quietly a while later.

"Not the will, I hope?"

"No. Maybe an even more sensitive issue. Your mother. And you."

Her gaze flickered up to meet his. "I know you noticed I was uncomfortable when Addy McGraw was asking questions about Brigit and me. I guess that Lincoln told you that my mother's and my relationship is…strained?"

Nick nodded.

"Mom kept her affair with Lincoln and my paternity secret, both from Derry and me. I haven't really spoken to her for most of my adult life," she admitted, feeling the familiar mixture of defiance and hurt rise up in her. "I realized when we were out there at McGraw Stables that Brigit never shared her love of horses with us because of her guilt. She associated horses with Lincoln and her infidelity."

"Were you and your mother close, before you had the falling-out?" Nick asked as he rubbed her shoulder in a soothing gesture.

"I was close to both of my parents. I was a Kavanaugh," she stated, as if that explained everything. "And then one summer evening when I was seventeen years old, I found out I wasn't."

His caressing hand stilled. Tears burned her eyes. She pressed her cheek to Nick's chest, averting her gaze.

"You mean you somehow found out about Brigit and Lincoln's affair?"

Deidre nodded, her cheek brushing against the springy hair on Nick's chest. She touched his skin with her fingertips, the sensation reassuring her…grounding her. Suddenly, the story was pouring out of her, as if it'd been waiting to erupt there at the back of her throat for nearly half of her life.

"When I was a kid, I thought my parents had the perfect marriage. They always seemed so happy, so attracted to each other. I had no way of knowing that apparently their marriage had started out rocky. Derry'd had an affair early on, and my mother had discovered it. She reacted by flying to Lake Tahoe and having an affair with her old friend, Lincoln Du-Bois. My mom and dad reconciled. All of us kids were happily ignorant of the whole thing, but one night when I was a teenager here in Harbor Town, the truth came spilling out."

She swallowed thickly and continued.

"I'd had a water-skiing accident during an exhibition show here in Harbor Town. I was hospitalized for a leg wound. It wasn't all that serious, but I'd lost some blood. I required a transfusion. That's how my dad—Derry—found out my blood type. He suspected that given his blood type, I couldn't biologically be his daughter. According to my brother Liam, Derry contacted an old friend after that—a pediatrician who specialized in genetic diseases. The pediatrician confirmed that given our blood types, I couldn't possibly be Derry's daughter.

"I was discharged from the hospital. Mom and I were the only two people in the house on Sycamore Avenue that afternoon. I remember it was a hot, humid summer evening. A storm broke that night. You could feel it brewing in the air all day. I was bored out of my mind. I could hear Mom doing dishes in the kitchen and figured the coast was clear to get out of bed and call one of my friends on the phone in my room. When I heard Mom coming upstairs a few minutes later, I thought I was caught, but she passed my room and went to hers and Dad's bedroom. A few minutes passed, and I heard the door downstairs open and close, and another tread on the stairs. I told my friend I had to get off the phone.

I recognized my father's step, and I was surprised he was home. It was a Tuesday, and Dad usually worked in Chicago until Thursday night, when he joined us in Harbor Town during the summers. He paused outside my door—I almost called out to him—I *wish* I had—but then I heard him walking down the hallway toward their bedroom.

"I don't know why I did it exactly—they would be mad at me for getting out of bed—but I got my crutches and left my room anyway. There was something really strange about Dad coming home. The atmosphere in the house seemed charged. I wanted to see Dad, to make sure everything was okay, even if I did get in trouble. I loved him so much…."

Nick cradled the back of her head with his hand and kissed the top of her head. "You don't have to go on if it's too upsetting to you," he said gruffly. She realized belatedly that she'd dropped into a whisper and finally faded off as she told her story.

"No. I want to tell you," she said, her voice stronger now. She'd never done this before, never spoken aloud the details of the night that had changed her life forever. She'd told some of the crucial details to Lincoln, but had kept things brief out of respect for his weakened condition and his profound love for Brigit Kavanaugh.

"The door was partially open to my parents' bedroom," she continued. "It didn't take long for me to recognize I shouldn't go barging in there. My dad wasn't shouting, but I'd never heard him sound the way he did that night. Tense. Desperate. I remember the tone of his voice scared me, even before I understood the details of what he was saying."

A thought occurred to her and she lifted her head, staring at Nick's shadowed face. "I was going to say, 'do you know what it's like to hear something and feel like your entire world was just yanked away from beneath your feet?' and then I realized of course you know exactly how that feels. You lost your parents."

He reached up and slid his thumb across her cheek, drying her tears. His serious, compassionate expression gave her the courage she required to continue.

"I listened to my father accusing my mother of having an affair. I heard him telling her that I couldn't be his biological daughter and he sounded so hurt…like he was wild with the pain of it. He didn't say anything about Marc, Colleen or Liam. Just *me,*" she said in a pressured whisper. She put her cheek back on Nick's chest. "*I* couldn't be my father's daughter. Then, my mother admitted there was a chance it was true."

"You must have been so confused…shocked."

"I felt like I was dreaming."

"But your mother didn't mention she'd had an affair with Lincoln DuBois specifically?"

Deidre shook her head. "All she said was there was a chance I was another man's child. Then my father told her in no uncertain terms there wasn't just a chance. His and my blood types proved it as an unassailable fact. I didn't know the identity of my biological father until Liam completed his investigation last summer. I've learned since that my mom told my father the name of the man she'd had an affair with on that night, but that was after I'd fled the scene. I asked my mother afterward. Many times. She refused to tell me my natural father's identity for all these years."

"It must have devastated you, hearing that as a kid," Nick said.

"I was confused. Disoriented. I remember I went back to my room and just lay there, staring up at the ceiling. I heard my father leave and thought I should do something. Go and demand the truth from my mother…something. But I was numb. Scared. I didn't want to believe it was true. Being a

Kavanaugh was such a central part of my identity. I adored my father. I couldn't comprehend what was happening to me…my family…the whole structure of my life.

"I eventually couldn't stand it anymore, lying there helpless. I grabbed my crutches and my keys and headed out. My mother heard me leaving, but I had a head start on her. I got in my car and drove. I'm not even sure where I went that night, but I had to get away. I learned later that my mother had also driven the streets and country roads, looking for both of us—Derry and me."

She paused, lost in her memories. "I eventually returned home…but my dad never did."

Nick's body tensed beneath hers. She felt the pressure of his hand on her chin and she lifted her head to meet his stare.

"Do you mean to tell me that was the same night as the accident? Your father died *that* night?"

She nodded. Pain tightened his features.

"Ah, Deidre…" he muttered, his voice thick with regret and compassion. He drew her tighter into his embrace and held her while she wept.

Later, after her tears ebbed, he laid her on her back and leaned over her. He kissed her cheeks, drying her tears. His lips on her mouth were tender as well, but Deidre laced her fingers through the hair at his nape and deepened the kiss, needing his passion at that moment…starved for it.

He lifted his head after a while and stared down at her. "You must have felt orphaned on that night," he said.

"I don't want to compare my experience to yours, but I did feel orphaned, in many ways," she admitted.

He nodded once. "You're not alone, Deidre. You're not alone."

She watched his dark head, spellbound, as he leaned down to kiss the upper curve of her right breast. He opened his mouth over the turgid crest. Pleasure and warmth inundated her. His tongue laved her nipple, and the sad memories scattered to the periphery of her consciousness. Only the present existed…and Nick.

She sighed his name and surrendered to the magic of his touch.

After they'd made love again, Nick drifted off to sleep, his head resting on her chest, his arms surrounding her. Deidre lay there for a while, drowsy and transfixed by the sensation of his warm, even breath on her breast.

After a while, she very carefully extricated herself from his arms, taking pains not to awaken him. She grabbed her robe and quietly left the bedroom. The forms for the Vivicor acquisition lay exactly where Nick had tossed them on the coffee table.

She bit at the top of the pen, hesitant for only a moment, before she placed the tip to the paper and signed her name.

Deidre awoke the next morning slowly, swimming in a sea of drowsy, sensual lassitude.

She smiled, her eyes still closed, when she recalled last night in vivid detail. She'd returned to bed after signing the forms and drifted off to sleep with Nick's scent in her nose. In the middle of the night, she'd been awakened by his touch. They'd lost themselves in one another again. Nick made love like he was reputed to do business. He was astonishingly patient at times, demanding and relentless at others, so brilliantly talented at his task that it made her toes curl beneath the sheets to remember.

She quickly turned over, both nervous and eager to see the man she'd grown so close to during the night in the light of dawn. Her heart seemed to drop an inch in her chest cavity when she realized she was alone in bed.

"Nick?" she called.

Something about the flat, answering silence told her she was utterly alone in the cottage. Where had he gone? She scooted to the opposite side of the bed when she saw a note propped against the lamp. She quickly scanned the note written in a narrow, slanting hand.

You were sleeping so soundly, I didn't have the heart to wake you.

I noticed you signed the papers. You didn't have to do that, but thanks. I need to fly up to Detroit for a meeting, but I'll be back late this afternoon. Will you have dinner with me at The Embers tonight? Seven o'clock? I'll pick you up at six forty-five.

Nick

P.S. I should feel guilty about keeping you up last night when I know how much you need your rest, but I'll admit I'm having a hell of a hard time regretting it.

Deidre smiled. She sprang out of bed, suddenly feeling as energetic and cheerful as a sixteen-year-old girl on the morning of her first date.

The first thing she did when she walked into the living room was turn on the lights on the Christmas tree. The second thing was turn on some holiday music. Not even her doubts about the wisdom of sleeping with Nick—of exposing her soul to him—could dampen her mood.

She took a hot shower; dressed in jeans, a fitted T-shirt and a flannel shirt; and called Colleen at the Family Center.

"I have a clothing emergency," Deidre said.

"Clothing emergency?"

"Yes. I need something to wear to dinner tonight at The Embers," she said, referring to the upscale restaurant in the Starling Hotel.

"Are you talking about a date?" Colleen demanded.

"I'll tell you about it later," Deidre mumbled. Colleen had insinuated she should consider Nick as more than her adversary. Deidre was a little embarrassed to admit to her sister just how drastically she'd altered her viewpoint of Nick. Maybe Colleen would be concerned that she'd taken things too far.

They arranged to meet at Colleen's house during her lunch hour. She said goodbye to her sister and was hanging up her phone when she heard a knock on the front door.

Her heart lurched with excitement. Had Nick decided not to go to Detroit? The knock came again. It wasn't Nick's bold knock, Deidre realized, but a crisp, feminine one.

"Mom," she mouthed soundlessly when she saw Brigit Kavanaugh standing on the porch.

Chapter Seven

Brigit smiled. "I thought I better come and see you in person. Apparently, you're not much of a phone person," her mother said, arching her eyebrows.

Deidre stepped back and waved her mother inside. She studied her unobtrusively as she took her coat and hung it. Brigit looked healthy and vibrant dressed in a dark blue sweater and a scarf with gray dress pants. Her mother had always been chic and effortlessly lovely, but her health had recently been a source of concern for her sons and daughters. When Marc had told her about Brigit's mild heart attack last year, Deidre had had a wild urge to jump on a plane and return to Michigan. To this day, Deidre didn't know if she hadn't because she was still angry or because she was afraid she wouldn't know what to say to her mother after all these years.

"Would you like a cup of tea?" Deidre asked awkwardly.

"Yes, thank you."

"Please, sit down," Deidre said, nodding toward the breakfast nook.

"Odd that it should come to this," Brigit said with a small smile. "Mother and daughter, talking to one another like acquaintances."

Deidre paused in the action of filling the teakettle. "Odd? Maybe. Understandable though."

"You were a girl when you left Harbor Town," Brigit said, twisting in her chair to face Deidre. "You're a woman, now. Surely time has given some perspective to your hurt about what you discovered on the night of Derry's death. Or maybe I can't help but be hopeful that it has."

Deidre set the teapot on the lit stove and approached Brigit slowly. "Are you suggesting that my anger at learning that I wasn't Derry's daughter was the melodramatics of a teenager, Mom? Dad died later that night because he'd discovered the same thing. Dad was a grown man, tough as nails. He was *destroyed* by that news."

"No…no, of course I'm not suggesting that," Brigit hurried to say. Her elegant throat convulsed as she swallowed. She waved toward a chair. "Sit down, Deidre. We haven't spoken to one another in private for a long, long time."

"Not since the night before I left Harbor Town, the night you refused to tell me my biological father's name," Deidre agreed, a hint of a challenge in her tone. Nevertheless, she sat down at the table next to her mother, her backbone rigid. Brigit met her stare and gave her a trembling smile.

"You have no idea now happy I was to see you at Liam and Natalie's dress rehearsal," she said feelingly.

"You shouldn't assume anything by it beyond the obvious. I came for Liam's wedding."

Brigit shook her head slowly. "No, Deidre."

"What do you mean, *no?*"

Brigit placed her hand on top of hers. It felt soft and warm next to her skin…a kind touch, a mother's touch. "We may be acting like strangers, but that's a lie. You're my daughter. I know you as well as I know my own name. Don't you think I remember how fierce you can be, and yet how generous?"

A band seemed to tighten around Deidre's throat. She didn't know if she was generous or forgiving. She didn't know *what* she was.

"Remember Leslie Warden?" Brigit asked.

Deidre blinked, surprised by the question and the name from the far past.

"She and her friends bullied you nonstop one summer between your third and fourth grade year. You stood up for yourself, though. You never backed down. And when Leslie pushed too hard one day, you gave her a bloody nose," Brigit recalled, caressing her hand.

"You and Dad grounded me for three weeks when you found out," Deidre remembered in a tight voice.

"We found out because you confessed it to us. You were beyond regretful. You were distraught. Between your sobs, Derry and I finally figured out that you were horrified you'd caused all that blood…all that pain. After that, you made it your mission to make things right with Leslie Warden. Your father and I never said a word to you about it. We didn't have to. You were fixed and determined about making up with that girl. And you did. The two of you were friends after that for years, even though she was a Harbor Town year-rounder and you only came during the summers. You may be fierce in your anger, Deidre, but you also possess one of the most forgiving spirits I've ever known. You wouldn't have returned to Harbor Town if you wanted this rift between us to continue."

"A lot can change about a person in half a lifetime," Deidre said, holding her mother's stare. "Circumstances can stretch a person's ability for forgiveness beyond tolerance."

"Like Lincoln's death, for instance?"

"Like Lincoln's death after I'd only had the chance to know him for three months," Deidre corrected. The teakettle began to whine. Her mother leaned toward her, her blue eyes moist.

"I can't change it, Deidre. I've wished I'd done things differently a thousand times over since you left Harbor Town. I've made myself sick with regrets. I know you probably don't want to hear it, but I thought I was doing what was best for you and Derry. Think of the heartache I'd have caused by confessing about the affair."

"That may have been true until I was a teenager, Mom, but what about after Dad died? I can't *believe* you were *never* planning to tell me the identity of my biological father. You knew Lincoln would have wanted to know me," she burst out heatedly.

"I considered telling you, but you've refused to speak to me all these years. You wouldn't come home. When I understood from your brothers and sister that you'd never revealed to them what you'd overheard on the night Derry and I argued, I assumed I was doing what you would have wanted by not speaking of it. I thought that *my* secret had become *yours*."

Deidre just stared, taken aback by her mother's pressured admission.

Brigit leaned back in her chair and gave a sigh thick with regret. "I caused worse heartache by having things come out the way they did," Brigit continued in a quieter tone. "I *know* that. I have to live with that—knowing I hurt you and Derry and Lincoln. I live with that every day, every hour. I'm not asking you to alleviate that pain, because no one can. That's my burden to bear."

"Lincoln forgave you," Deidre blurted out, surprising herself.

Brigit nodded slowly.

"You knew?" Deidre whispered.

"He contacted me after you went to his house in South Lake and told him what Liam had discovered."

"What did Lincoln say?"

"Just what you said. That he forgave me for what I'd done. And that…"

"What?" Deidre prompted when Brigit's voice faded.

"That he wanted to see me again," said Brigit, now staring out the breakfast nook windows toward the vast lake.

"Did you? See him again?" Deidre asked, dazed. Surely she would have known if her mother had come to The Pines while she was there.

Brigit blinked and met her stare. "I never spoke with Lincoln. Not once since I left him years ago in Lake Tahoe. I never broke that vow to myself. He left a message on my answering machine at the house a few months back. That's how I knew he'd forgiven me."

"You *wanted* to see him, didn't you?"

"Of course I did," Brigit replied with a sad smile.

"Why didn't you go then?"

Brigit sighed, seeming to search for the words. It struck Deidre her mother was having difficulty expressing herself because she'd never spoken her feelings aloud.

How lonely she must be.

"Lincoln was my dear friend. He loved me unconditionally. I didn't deserve that. Not after I refused to see him again and reconciled with Derry. Not after I'd deprived him of you."

Deidre stared. Her mother was saying she believed it was her punishment to be deprived of the unconditional love of a man who had always adored her. Part of Deidre agreed with Brigit's self-imposed penance. Another part ached for her mother so much it nearly stole her breath.

Brigit touched her hand again. "Something Lincoln said

in the message he left a few months back made me think he'd accepted you as his child."

"He did," Deidre whispered. "He's made me his heir, to his fortune and to his company, along with Nick Malone."

Brigit gasped.

"You truly loved Lincoln, didn't you?" Deidre asked, reading the truth in her mother's startled expression and haunted eyes.

Brigit gripped at her hand, and Deidre found herself clutching back this time. "I loved both Derry and Lincoln, but not in the same way. Derry was my soul mate, my only true love. But Lincoln was unwaveringly loyal, the dearest friend of my heart. He understood me, maybe better than Derry ever could. It would have been a comfort to bask in Lincoln's love and forgiveness. But it just wasn't meant to be.

"What's between us is different, Deidre," Brigit said after a tense silence.

"How so?"

"I could punish myself further by forsaking the incomparable treasure of a daughter. Maybe I would, if it weren't for one thing. You need me. I can't imagine how distraught you must be feeling following Lincoln's death, and then to find out this huge thing—that he's made you his heir. You must be overwhelmed," Brigit said feelingly. "A mother is the thing that grounds us, reminds us of who we are. I know I haven't been that for you for a long, long time, but I want to be that for you again, Deidre. I've never known a young woman who needed a loving mother more. And I do love you," she said hoarsely, her gaze entreating. "Please know that. I feel like a part of myself was cut away when you left my life all those years ago."

Emotion swelled in Deidre, clogging her throat. She stood abruptly, but Brigit tightened her hold on her hand, halting her.

"You returned to Harbor Town. Isn't everything we had before all the tragedy enough for us to at least begin talking again? I know I'm far from perfect. I've made terrible mistakes. But you're my daughter. I'm your mother. Can't we try to start anew?"

The teakettle continued to wail. Deidre started and swiped her hand over a damp cheek. She broke contact with her mother and moved toward the stove.

"At least agree to come for Christmas," Brigit said. "Please?"

Deidre turned off the gas burner and reached for two cups, hardly aware of what she was doing.

"I've upset you. I'll pass on the tea for now," Brigit said quietly after a moment. Deidre paused in her senseless task of making tea and glanced at her mother over her shoulder. Brigit had stood and retrieved her coat. "Will you at least *think* about coming to Sycamore Avenue for Christmas?"

Deidre looked away, moved by the naked longing she'd seen on her mother's face.

"I'll think about it," she said. She stilled beneath Brigit's soft touch on her shoulder. A moment later, she heard the front door close quietly.

After her mother's visit, she felt drained. Colleen noted her preoccupation later when they met at her house for lunch, mistaking it for exhaustion.

"You seem tired. I thought you said you were feeling much better when we spoke on the phone earlier," Colleen said as she led Deidre to her bedroom.

"I am. It's just…Mom stopped by the cottage earlier."

Colleen paused in the entry to her bedroom, her expression tense. "She did? How did it go? Not very well, from the looks of things."

Deidre waved her hand. "You can't really expect a meeting like that to go *well,* can you? Maybe it's enough that it went at all."

Colleen gave her an understanding glance. "All right. I get it. You don't want to talk about it right now."

"Suffice it to say that Mom asked me to spend Christmas on Sycamore Avenue, and I didn't say no."

Colleen's brows arched appraisingly. "Now that *is* something." She opened her mouth to say something else, but seemed to reconsider. She swept across the room to her closet. "But so is this date tonight with Nick Malone. We better focus on that."

"Thank you for helping me. I'm a fashion disaster. I haven't bought any new clothes since I first moved to Germany. I hate shopping," Deidre explained as Colleen started pulling dresses off the rack.

Colleen laughed from the interior of her walk-in closet.

"What's so funny?"

"Sorry." Colleen grinned. "It just struck me as funny. An heiress who hates to shop."

"I'll be kicked out of the billionaire's club for sure," Deidre mumbled, rolling her eyes.

"Here. I have the perfect dress. It always ran small on me, but it'll be just right for you."

She admired the sophisticated black knit Colleen showed her.

"I'll even throw in a pair of heels and earrings if you tell me one thing," Colleen offered.

"Yes?"

"Are you falling for Nick Malone?"

Heat flooded her cheeks. She hadn't been prepared for the blunt question, but she should have been, given it was Colleen doing the asking.

"I suppose you'd think I was a fool if I was," Deidre said,

holding up the dress and eyeing herself in the vanity mirror, trying to avoid Colleen's stare.

"I'd think you were a fool if you weren't," Colleen corrected crisply. "Not a fool, actually. More like a robot or something. There's no way a woman wouldn't be affected by having a man that looks like Nick stare at her the way he stares at you. While we were in Tahoe, you showed a real flair for avoiding Nick. But on the phone this morning, you sounded practically giddy at the idea of a date with him. Something's going on between you two. Something major."

Colleen's knowing glance informed Deidre she might as well forget dissembling. She sighed and tossed the dress on the bed. "All right. I'm…interested in him." Her cheeks heated even more when she noticed Colleen's arch expression. "Okay, I'm *really* interested. Am I crazy? Getting involved with Nick Malone, of all people? He may end up taking me to court. I don't know up from down anymore. When did my life become so complicated? The most difficult thing used to be doing a week of night-shift duty. I'm not sure if Nick even trusts me completely."

"He wants you though."

"As if that matters."

"Do you trust him?" Colleen challenged.

"Yes." She met Colleen's stare. "More than I ever have before. I think he's been up front with me from the beginning. I may not have liked what he's been saying, but at least he's been honest."

Colleen smiled and walked over to her closet. She turned around with a pair of sexy black heels dangling from her fingers.

"Remember. Fate favors the bold," she said.

Deidre made a face. She'd told Colleen the same thing when her sister had shown up at The Pines, heartbroken and avoiding Eric Reyes. "Okay, I may be simplifying things a little out of proportion to the complexities of the situation," Colleen admitted, handing Deidre the heels. "So I'll just stick with *good luck*."

"Thanks, I think I'm going to need it."

"You used to jump two hundred and fifty feet off ski ramps. You've been known to run into a bullet fray to rescue a patient. You can do anything. You're my big sister," Colleen added the last fondly, as if it explained everything.

She laughed and hugged Colleen. "Thank you. Maybe I wouldn't choose the bullets over Nick, but I have to wonder which situation is more dangerous."

"Nobody ever said love was simple."

Deidre's mouth fell open. *"Love?"*

Colleen shrugged and hid her grin by starting to search for the promised pair of earrings.

Later that evening Deidre recalled her insinuation that Nick Malone was potentially dangerous. She turned to the side and examined herself in the full-length mirror behind the bathroom door.

She was the one who looked dangerous. Forget "little black dress." The number Colleen had loaned her was downright racy.

Not that it was indecent by any means. It wasn't low-cut and it covered her knees. In fact, it was quite elegant. It was more the way it hugged every curve she possessed that made her eyes go wide when she appraised herself. The sexy black pumps did a lot for her legs. Even her small breasts looked somehow…*significant* in the molding knit fabric of the dress, she realized in rising panic.

She twisted around and examined herself from the back. *Oh, no.* The dress gently cupped her hips and bottom, leaving little to the imagination. At the top, it dipped in an oval, leaving her upper back exposed. The conservative pearls and earrings she wore only seemed to emphasize the sexiness of the dress by contrast.

Nick would think she was… She didn't know *what* Nick would think. He was used to seeing her in jeans and T-shirts and boots.

She raced to her bedroom, intent on changing into something else—a frumpy skirt and blouse, if need be. *Anything*, as long as Nick wouldn't think she was playing the sex siren.

His bold knock sounded at the front door.

Deidre paused in the action of whipping a blouse off a hanger. She stared at the garment in rising panic. It was totally unsuitable for dinner at The Embers. She tossed the blouse on her bed and placed her hand on her chest, willing her pounding heartbeat to slow.

Get a grip, Kavanaugh.

She was a grown woman. It wasn't even as if she hadn't slept with Nick yet. She had no excuse for hysterics.

"Hi," she said a moment later when she opened the front door. He stood on the front porch, looking incredibly handsome in his black overcoat, a white shirt and silk tie showing through the opening.

"Hi."

She blushed furiously when she noticed his stare run over her from brow to toe. His expression looked flat…stunned? She couldn't have felt more exposed than if she had answered the door stark naked.

He entered and she shut the door. She hastened to get her coat and cover up the dress. He halted her by grabbing her hand and pulling her into his arms.

"You look outrageously beautiful," he said with quiet intensity.

"Thank you," she whispered. "You look nice, too."

A puzzled expression flickered across his face. "Am I being punished for leaving a note this morning?"

Deidre blinked in surprise. "Punished? No, of course not. What do you mean?"

"You seem kind of distant," he said, his gaze scanning her face. "I thought maybe you were mad about the note. I'm sorry—I really did think it was better to let you sleep. I wanted to wake you up. Trust me on that."

She flushed in pleasure.

"Oh, no. I'm not upset by that at all." When he just continued to study her somberly, Deidre felt she should explain. "I'm just a little…embarrassed."

He quirked one eyebrow. Deidre became distracted by the sensation of him lightly circling her hips in his palms. "Why are you embarrassed?"

She ducked her head. "I don't usually wear dresses like this, that's all. I hadn't realized when I borrowed it from Colleen it was quite so…"

"Sexy as hell?" Her gaze shot up to his. A small grin tugged at his mouth. "It only is because you're in it."

She gave a shaky smile.

"Deidre?"

"Yes?"

"I've been looking forward to seeing you again ever since I shut your bedroom door this morning. I was sort of hoping for a little bit more of a warm welcome, after last night," he murmured, pulling her closer.

"Were you?" she asked softly, her embarrassment fading to mist. Feeling Nick next to her made her forget almost everything. She went up on her toes, letting her body slide against his. His nostrils flared slightly as he stared down at her. His hold on her hips tightened and suddenly she was airborne. He sat her on the kitchen counter and swooped down to kiss her.

And what a kiss.

It was so hot, so demanding she felt a delicious sensation curl tight in the pit of her stomach and tickle the tips of her breasts. He brought her closer. She looped her arms around his neck and kissed him back with all the passion he'd awakened in her last night.

A minute later, he sealed their kiss and pressed his forehead to hers. Deidre panted softly, inhaling his aromatic aftershave.

"Was that more of what you had in mind for a welcome?" she asked.

"Yeah, but it might have been a little too good," he mumbled as he plucked at her lips. "Do you want to skip dinner?"

She ran her fingers through the hair at his collar and slid her lips next to his sensually. "Okay. But you might never see me dressed up like this again."

He paused in his kissing. "I can't wait to get you *out* of the dress, to be honest. But maybe you're right," he said grimly before he lifted her and set her feet back on the ground. He kissed her once on the forehead and once on the lips. "Come on, let's go. Before I change my mind."

"Are you sure?" Deidre asked when he turned to get her coat.

"No. But what kind of a heel would I be if I took you straight to bed after all the trouble you took dressing for dinner?"

"I really don't care," Deidre admitted as he slid on her coat.

"I do," he said simply before he opened the door for her and took her hand.

"How are we doing?" Nick asked her after the waiter had cleared the remains of their dinner and served them coffee. They sat in an intimate booth. The candle on the table flickered in the reflection from the windowpane next to them.

"How are we doing with what?" Deidre wondered.

"How are we doing with ignoring everything but each other's company?"

She smiled as she poured a splash of cream into her coffee. "I'd say we're doing fantastic. I'm having a wonderful time," she said, meaning it. Nick was excellent company—smart without being overbearing, an encyclopedia of knowledge and experience, funny in a no-nonsense, dry sort of way, extremely handsome in his well-cut suit and tie. He'd listened intently while she'd described her meeting with her mother that morning. It surprised her a little that she ended up telling him much more about the emotional encounter than she had Colleen.

She studied him from beneath lowered lashes as she stirred her coffee. Could a woman sustain herself solely by eating up the vision of his rugged male glory? She mused. She was quite sure she wasn't the first woman to wonder such a thing.

He did a double take when he noticed her grin.

"Why the smile?"

She shrugged and took a sip of her coffee. "Colleen showed me some photos online of you at charity events and so forth."

"I'm hardly a society butterfly. Those damn photographers would spring up on me on the way to the office mail room if I gave them the opportunity," he mumbled, looking a little sheepish at her choice of topic.

She hid her smile. "I couldn't help but notice that none of the women you were escorting ever showed up more than once."

He raised his eyebrows. "Oh. So you're wondering if I ever get serious about a woman, is that it?"

She met his gaze across the table. "I'm getting the impression you're one of the Great Uncatchables."

He stared out the window. For the first time since she'd known him, she got the impression Nick was uncomfortable. "I've had a couple relationships that fit into the 'serious' category."

"What went wrong?" she asked with a small, mischievous smile.

"Nothing at all. The relationships just weren't meant to be in the long run." He leaned back and placed his arm along the back of the booth, examining her. "Are you ribbing me?"

She laughed, taken aback by his blunt question. His mouth tilted in amusement. Seeing his smile caused a rush of warmth to go through her.

"Believe it or not, I am. I tend to tease a lot. You've only been a witness to my grouchy side in the past, unfortunately."

His smile lingered on his lips. "I used to hear you sometimes before I'd enter Linc's room and you were with him," he said quietly. "I was a little shocked that the prickly female I always seemed to encounter was the same teasing, charming one I heard talking to Linc."

Their gazes clung.

"I'll admit to being a little jealous," he said. "What about you though. I've sort of gotten the impression you're one of the Great Uncatchables yourself."

"Don't be ridiculous," she said, laughing. She toyed with her water goblet. "There was one man," she admitted after a pause.

His smile faded.

"You don't know about him?" she asked cautiously. "I thought maybe from your background investigation…"

He frowned and tossed his napkin onto the table. "I recall two or three names of men you'd dated, but the man who reported to me didn't make it sound like anything serious. I didn't realize that only one of the men would have qualified as an answer to my question," he replied.

"His name was David Sandoff. He was a navy surgeon.

And as it turned out, he didn't really qualify as a serious re-lationship at all."

"What makes you say that?"

"Oh, probably the fact that I found out he had a fiancée in Brooklyn the whole time he was with me," she said, smiling ruefully. She glanced up from fiddling with her dessert fork.

"What an ass," he said.

"You took the words right out of my mouth," she mur-mured, flattered by his irritation. "It was all for the best. My dramatic discovery coincided with my tour of duty ending in Afghanistan. I moved to Germany days later," she said, shaking her head in disgust at the memory.

"Do you think if he hadn't been an unfaithful jerk, some-thing might have come from the relationship?"

She shrugged. "I doubt it, to be honest. My brother Marc says I have wanderlust. I don't like to stay in one place too long."

"You don't want to settle down," he clarified.

She looked at him. "People usually want to settle down in a place they can call home."

For a moment, neither of them spoke.

"You have The Pines now to call home," he said quietly. "You have Harbor Town, too, if you choose it. It sounds to me like your mother would agree with me on that."

She gave a polite smile as the waiter approached with their dessert, glad for the distraction to mask her uncertainty.

It was a clear, cold night when they left the restaurant. Stars packed the night sky. Nick asked her if she was up for a drive, and Deidre agreed. They coasted down Buena Vista Drive, admiring the Christmas lights on the luxurious lake-front homes. Afterward, they went past the harbor and down Main Street, where cheerful lights and festive decorations adorned the park, shops and lampposts. Deidre was so comfortable in their conversation, it took her a moment to realize where Nick was turning a few minutes later.

"Oh…wait. This is Sycamore Avenue," she exclaimed. "You're not planning on—"

"It's a pretty street. I like these old, established neighborhoods," he said, driving the car at a snail's pace. "I thought a trip down Sycamore Avenue might coax a memory or two from you. It'll help me to get to know you better." She caught the gleam in his eyes when he glanced over at her reprovingly. "Don't worry. I'm not taking you to your mom's. I wouldn't share you tonight with anyone in the world."

"Okay," Deidre said, relieved Nick wasn't suggesting they march up and knock at her mother's front door. She was getting more comfortable with the idea of spending time with Brigit, but the idea of entering the house again intimidated her for some reason. "You *really* want to accompany me on a trip down memory lane?" she asked with a doubtful grin.

"Maybe not a whole trip, but a few snippets might be nice."

She chuckled and glanced out the window. Sycamore Avenue looked like the front of a Christmas card on the frosty night. All of the neighbors who had decorated must have decided communally to use white lights and fresh greenery.

She leaned forward and pointed through the front window at the wooded cul de sac at the end of the street. "There's an entrance to Sycamore Avenue Beach and the lakefront walk just through there. My brothers and sister and I practically camped out on the beach there during the summer. We dreaded the sound of our parents calling us home for dinner. Every August all the Sycamore Avenue neighbors used to gather for a huge barbecue down at the beach. My dad always manned an enormous grill, and the neighbor ladies gave him everything to cook from hamburgers to shish kebab to fresh vegetables out of their gardens. Mari's father—Mr. Itani— made enough homemade ice cream to make us kids think we'd died and gone to heaven. He'd always try to surprise us with at least one exotic new flavor a year. My favorite was pistachio, so he made it for me every August. He was such a sweet man." She smiled wistfully in memory. "At dusk, the adults would dance on the beach. My parents were always the best dancers of all," she added, surprising herself when she heard the note of pride in her voice.

She pointed to the left of the street. "That was my friend Grace Schetel's house, and there's Mari's family's old house."

"No old boyfriends used to live on Sycamore?"

She shook her head with mock somberness. "No such luck."

He chuckled. "There's a story there, I'm thinking."

"I had a huge, unrequited crush on Mari's older brother, Ryan. But that was nothing unusual. Half the girls in Harbor Town did." They slowly approached the attractive white, colonial revival house on the right. She pointed to her mother's house. "There's the summer house. My bedroom was the corner one facing the street. I think I spent almost two entire weeks during my thirteenth summer in that window there, staring down Sycamore Avenue, waiting for Ryan Itani to come home on his motorcycle. I was heartbroken he didn't know I existed."

Nick gave her a wry sideways glance. "I find it hard to believe a guy didn't know you existed."

"Quite a normal phenomenon for a skinny as a rail thirteen-year-old girl, trust me," Deidre assured, grinning.

Nick turned the sedan off Sycamore Avenue a few minutes later. Deidre reached out and touched his thigh.

"Thanks," she said when he glanced over at her.

"For what?"

"For reminding me that while there are a lot of sad memories associated with that street, there were even more wonderful ones."

As they returned to Cedar Cottage, Deidre coaxed him into talking about his parents.

"They're all good memories of your mom and dad, even though they died when you were so young," she said later as they pulled into the driveway. "You're lucky in that aspect."

"I am," Nick agreed as he put the car in Park.

"Is that part of why you didn't want Lincoln to become a true father figure to you? Out of loyalty to your real father?" she asked in a hushed tone.

He kept his face turned in profile. "Maybe."

"It's confusing, isn't it?" she asked in a burst of honesty. "I feel so guilty at times, disloyal to my dad—Derry, I mean—because I wanted to know Lincoln so much. I feel guilty in regard to Lincoln, too. He might have been hurt if he knew when I think of 'Dad' I automatically think of Derry."

"I can't speak for Derry, but as far as Linc goes, I bet he would have understood completely."

Deidre nodded. "He had a huge heart," she murmured, thinking of what her mother had told her about Lincoln. "I wish my heart was so forgiving."

She turned when Nick touched her, sliding her chin into the palm of his hand. He caressed her ear with his fingertips. A powerful surge of sexual awareness went through her at his touch.

"I wouldn't sell yourself short on that," he said gruffly. "Even the most generous of hearts needs time to heal."

"Thank you," she whispered. "After seeing Mom today, I'm feeling a little more optimistic about things. Like…maybe the hardest part is over."

He touched his lips to hers. Deidre closed her eyes and ran her fingers through his hair. The kiss started slowly, their mouths teasing and molding. Nick's teeth lightly scraped at her lower lip and she sighed.

His tongue slid into her mouth and she was lost.

"Do you want to come inside?" she whispered shakily a minute later as he pressed his hot mouth to her neck.

"I thought you'd never ask," he replied.

Chapter Eight

Once they were inside the cottage, Nick whipped his coat off and draped it on a kitchen chair. Deidre was trying to unbutton her coat when he interrupted her by cradling her jaw in both of his hands and lifting her face. He seized her mouth in a searing kiss.

"I couldn't stop thinking about you all day long," he said a moment later as he helped her draw her coat off her arms. He laid it on top of his, took her hand and led her out of the kitchen.

"I couldn't stop thinking about you, either," Deidre admitted as she followed him. When they reached the bedroom, Nick switched on the bedside lamp to its dimmest setting. He drew her in front of him and began to unzip her dress. His breath came in uneven puffs of warm air against her neck.

"I hope you don't think this is crass," he mumbled as he brushed the dress over her shoulders, "but this first time might be short and sweet. I feel like the past twelve hours has been ten years, waiting to touch you again." He groaned when he pushed the dress down to her ankles and she stood wearing only a black bra, panties, thigh-high hose and heels. He ran his hand along her naked hip and stifled a groan. "God, you're beautiful. Better make that very fast and very furious." His glance at her was hot and entreating. "I'll make it up to you afterward. I promise."

Deidre laughed, flattered by his admission. She turned in his arms. "I believe you," she said truthfully. She went up on her toes and met him in a kiss. Their mouths clung when he lifted her against him and moved toward the bed, sitting heavily on the edge of the mattress. Deidre's knees parted as she straddled him. She couldn't get enough of the taste of him or the sensation of his molding lips and searching tongue. She shivered uncontrollably when he ran his hands over her from shoulder to hip. He placed both hands on her bottom and slid her closer into his lap. She moaned feverishly into his mouth when she felt the strength of his arousal.

No wonder he'd said things would be fast and furious.

Her sex clenched tight at the mere thought.

She became transported with heat…with need. She whispered his name as she rained kisses along his collar and began to tug at his tie. He helped her and she was free to unfasten his shirt. She opened the fabric a moment later and ran her hands over his chest and the erotic swell of his shoulder muscles. It felt so good she leaned down to sample the dense flesh with her teeth.

Nick hissed and his hold on her buttocks tightened. Deidre heard the hard edge of arousal in his tone, and it thrilled her. Her mouth moved over him hungrily, sampling his chest, tasting a small, rigid nipple. She felt feverish…liberated by her desire. She went lower, leaning down and tilting her head to scrape her teeth lightly against the side of a rib.

She began to unbuckle his belt, holding his gaze as she unfastened his trousers.

"Deidre," he grated out when she took his length into her hand. She wondered anew at how hard and heavy his erection felt against her palm and stroking fingers. His eyes seemed alight with need as he watched her through narrowed lids. "This is how you treat a man when he tells you he's hurting for you?"

"It's how I treat *you*," she whispered back in a quiet challenge. She braced herself with her hands on his thighs. She slid between his legs until her knees hit the carpet.

"Damn it, Deidre," he groaned when she took him in her hand again. He combed his fingers through her hair and cradled the back of her skull, the gesture gentle and possessive at once. He halted her from leaning forward.

She looked up at him, admiring the image of his lean, muscular torso between the opening of his white dress shirt, his tie draped around his shoulders. She recalled all too poignantly how she'd once considered him cold, relentless and calculating. He seemed the opposite of that in that moment. He seemed undone by desire, and she loved it.

"I want to," she told him, her lips moving but no sound coming from her mouth.

His jaw tightened and his nostrils flared. "Far be it from me to stop you then. But I'm going to get you back later."

"I look forward to it," she assured him before she leaned forward and tasted him.

A while later, Nick landed one last kiss along the softness of Deidre's thigh and rose over her. She lay naked on the bed, her head on the pillows. He was glad he'd left the light on. He wouldn't have wanted to miss the sublime expression on Deidre's face at that moment for the world. He lightly licked her upper lip and tasted her sweat, letting it blend with the essence of her on his tongue.

"So proud of yourself for getting back at me so well," she murmured with a hint of a smile. He dipped his tongue between her lips and heard her soft moan of renewed arousal.

Who had he been kidding? he wondered hazily as he plundered Deidre's mouth and she responded so wholly, so sweetly…without an ounce of reservation. He'd thought he could maintain at least some level of objectivity when it came to her, but that had been before he'd tasted her…before he felt the perfection of her deepest embrace.

This courageous, beautiful, wounded woman deserved only happiness, and he knew now he would never do anything to intentionally hurt her. But what if they discovered she wasn't really Lincoln DuBois's daughter? Would she blame him for the pain she felt if that were true? Would she blame him if he were honest with her about facts over which he had no control?

She arched against him, her breasts pressing against his chest. He answered her need wordlessly, gritting his teeth as he entered her, feeling her muscles clench around him, drawing him deeper, urging him into the center of her heat. He thrust and watched her face through a narrowed gaze, unable to look away from the image of Deidre's desire, of her acceptance of him.

It'd slice him deep if she withdrew that acceptance.

The thought of Deidre being alone in the world cut at him even worse.

The next morning was a gray, leaden day. Nick said he had a conference call with his San Francisco staff, so he rose and showered while Deidre snuggled in bed, missing his solid warmth. After Deidre had cleaned up, Nick lingered in the living room, sipping the coffee Deidre had made.

"I thought you needed to make a call at nine-thirty," Deidre reminded him.

"I do," he said, sitting down on the couch. "But I'll give them a call and tell them I'm running a few minutes late." He held out his arm and Deidre sat down next to him, her legs folded beneath her, her body curving into Nick's embrace like a pea in a pod. To her, he looked—and smelled—every bit as wonderful as he had last night wearing his dark gray suit. This morning, he even had the added bonus of a slightly disreputable, sexy scruff on his jaw.

"What are you grinning about?" he murmured, running his fingers through the still-damp hair at her nape. She shivered at his touch.

"I was thinking you really look the part of a corporate cowboy this morning."

"Is that a bad or good thing?"

"Oh…very good," she assured him before their lips met in a kiss.

"Do you want me to fill you in on what the meeting is about today? You can come and listen, if you like," he said a moment later, his forehead pressed against hers. "It wouldn't hurt for you to slowly start to absorb some of this stuff. It doesn't mean you have to do anything with it, but knowledge is always good, right?" he added when he leaned back and noticed her bewilderment.

"Right," she admitted. "Why don't you just fill me in?"

She listened with a tight focus while Nick gave the names and job titles of the people he would meet with this morning. Each man or woman was the president of a major DuBois global unit or subsidiary company. Deidre realized he was trying to begin to convey to her the overall structure of DuBois Enterprises. It began to dawn on her just how vast the corporation was.

"…real estate and development—Travis Moore, health

and agricultural sciences—Emmit Chandis, media—Melanie Marcraft, and computer and space technology—Spencer Jones," Deidre repeated back to him the major global units and their presidents a while later.

"Perfect score," Nick said before he checked his watch. "I really should get going. All the aforementioned people are going to be waiting for me." He glanced back at her as he stood. "If you want to learn more about DuBois Enterprises in general, why don't you just check things out on your laptop? The website has a pretty good overview."

Deidre stood along with him. "I know you'll find this hard to believe, but I don't own a laptap or iPad or anything remotely techy except for my cell phone." She saw his slightly stunned expression and blushed. "See? What did I tell you? I'm the last person Lincoln should have ever considered to co-run his company. I'm a twenty-first-century dinosaur, according to Colleen."

"I don't think a qualifier for the position is how many pieces of personal technology you own," Nick said.

"I should be getting the call pretty soon about the genetic testing," she said quietly as he put on his coat, voicing a thought that had been haunting her all morning.

His expression sobered. It was the first time since they'd become intimate with one another that they'd mentioned the genetic testing out loud.

"Yeah. I know."

The moment felt strained. Deidre was confused. Nick's faith in her seemed to be growing by the hour, but he still was worried about what they'd discover in regard to her paternity. The awkward silence proved that.

He reached out suddenly and cradled the side of her head. "I have a surprise for you."

"Another one?" she asked, laughing, thankful he'd broken the tension.

"It's not a huge one. It's really just an excuse for me to spend time with you this afternoon. Can I pick you up at around two?"

"Yes," she whispered, ensnared by his eyes.

He kissed her softly and then deeply enough to make her toes curl in her slippers and her fingers grip at the lapel of his coat.

The second the front door shut, she already missed him.

Deidre ate a late breakfast and took a call from her brother Marc. He had a recommendation for an attorney who specialized in estate law and contested wills.

"His name is Mike Bonella, and he has a national reputation as being one of the best. Malone will know of him, and he won't be so quick to try and take advantage of you if he knows you have Mike in your corner. Why don't you give Mike a call? He's very interested in speaking to you. Of course, in all honesty, there's not an estate lawyer in the country who wouldn't want to be retained for such a high-profile case," Marc admitted wryly.

The shell of euphoria surrounding Deidre after her night and morning with Nick started to crack at Marc's words. Reality started to leak in.

"Deidre? You okay?" Marc asked when she remained silent.

"Yes, I'm fine."

"Has Malone been giving you a hard time?"

"No, it's not that at all, it's just…" She bit her lower lip. Marc would kill her if she told him she'd been foolish enough to get romantically involved with Nick Malone. If she considered things from Marc's perspective, she *was* behaving idiotically. "I should hear any day now about the genetic testing. I guess I'm just hesitant to call a lawyer and make any big plans when my life is so uncertain right now."

She heard her brother sigh. "Yeah, well I guess it couldn't

hurt to wait a couple days. Although I'd prefer you at least had Mike Bonella's name behind you. Are you starting to get nervous? About the test results, I mean?"

"Starting? My nerves have been fried since before I even went for the testing. It just gets worse every day."

"I can imagine," Marc admitted.

"It's kind of stupid for me to be nervous, isn't it? I mean… it's not like Mom slept around. If she says my natural father was Lincoln DuBois, it was Lincoln DuBois, right?"

"Right," Marc said.

"So how come I still feel so nervous?"

"Probably because you know things will *really* start to get hairy when you discover for certain you are Lincoln's biological child."

Deidre wrote down the information about the lawyer, feeling unsettled the whole time. Her night and morning with Nick was still too vibrant in her memory—still singing in her flesh. The phone call with Marc had interrupted her happiness and made her question her loyalties. She thought of how Nick had begun teaching her some of the basics about DuBois this morning and how he'd recommended she contact Abel Warren, Lincoln's personal attorney. He was starting to support her, mentor her, even. But surely Nick would understand that she might need her own legal counsel, given the possibility of how things may unfold?

She glanced down at the piece of paper with Mike Bonella's number on it. If she ended up calling Bonella, it would be because Nick told her he was taking her to court. A sick, uneasy feeling grew in her stomach.

She dressed in a scarlet sweater and tucked her black skinny jeans into her tie-up snow boots. She took time styling her hair and with her makeup, trying to distract herself from her anxiety. Afterward, she ran a few errands and stopped by Liam's and Natalie's house to collect their mail.

Despite her eagerness to see Nick, nervousness started to twine with her anticipation as two o'clock approached. Her heart seemed to leap into her throat when she heard his car door slam in the driveway at a few minutes past two.

"Hey," he greeted when she opened the door and cold air rushed across her face.

Seeing his tall, shadowed form against the brilliant backdrop of the sunny winter day and glistening blue lake brought back every detail of last night. The passionate connection they'd made was special, wasn't it? Unique? It certainly had been in her experience.

He'd changed into jeans and boots. He stepped toward her, taking her in his arms. She realized she'd been gaping at him like she hadn't seen him in months instead of hours.

"Hi," she muttered, her gaze stuck on the dazzling sight of his dimples and sexy smile.

"You can do better than that," he murmured before he edged toward her, leaned down and kissed her. Deidre went up on her toes and improved her greeting enthusiastically. His grin was long gone by the time he lifted his head a moment later.

"I'm already regretting this."

"What?" Deidre asked, alarm spiking through the sensual lassitude wrought by his kiss.

He tilted his chin toward the driveway. "The plans I made. I'd much rather just take you back to bed."

"Why don't you then?" she asked, grinning. The idea of them losing themselves in each other and keeping the rest of the world at bay for as long as they could sounded very, very appealing.

His eyes were fixed on her mouth like he was considering taking another bite out of her, but then he was backing out of her arms. "I wish I could, but...well, come on. You'll see. I hope you don't kill me for it," he added under his breath.

"Nick, what are you talking about?" she asked, mystified by his behavior.

"It's a beautiful day—perfect for a tour of the area. Let's go up."

"Up?"

"Yeah. In my plane."

"Oh."

He smiled, obviously noticing her dubiousness. The flash of his white teeth took her off guard. As usual. He was usually so serious. When he smiled, she couldn't look away from him.

"I'm a good pilot. You can trust me."

"I do," she said softly. "Let me get my coat." She reached for her coat tree, but he reached it before her. She turned, and he slid it over her shoulders. A shiver went through her when he placed a kiss on her ear.

"You look beautiful."

"Thanks," she mumbled as she faced him, warmed by the heat of his stare.

She took his proffered hand, locking and slamming the door behind her. When they reached the corner of the cottage, he tugged slightly on her hand as if to get her attention. She paused.

"I meant well, Deidre," Nick said quietly.

"What?" Deidre asked, perplexed.

"I had the best intentions," he murmured. He nodded toward the driveway and spoke near Deidre's ear. "It was just a chance happening. I ran into her on Main Street. I'd rather have you to myself, but I can't take back the invitation now."

Deidre glanced toward Nick's car and froze. Her mother sat in the passenger seat of his sedan.

"I asked your mom to come up in the plane with us," Nick said.

* * *

Nick watched Deidre's face closely, seeing when the flicker of anxiety faded and was replaced by a beautiful mask. In the past, he'd been reminded of Joan of Arc when she leveled that fierce, cold, determined expression at him. Now, he was more struck by how quickly she donned the facade. How did she repress her anxiety so effortlessly?

He urged her toward his car. He opened the passenger door and Brigit stepped out and warmly kissed her daughter on the cheek. Deidre grasped Brigit's elbows as she stiffly returned the greeting.

"No, Mom, I'll get in the back," Deidre insisted when Brigit started to get in the backseat.

Deidre pointedly avoided his gaze when he opened the door for her. He suppressed his regret as he walked around to the driver's side. Deidre may be irritated at his heavy-handedness in the short term, but he still thought trying to bridge the rift between mother and daughter was the right thing to do in the long run.

"Well, this is certainly a surprise," Deidre said as Nick backed out of the driveway. He briefly met Deidre's eyes in the rearview mirror. Her frosty glance assured him this wasn't the type of surprise she'd anticipated this morning when he'd mentioned it.

"For me, too." Brigit laughed. "I ran into Nick this morning as I was leaving Celino's Bakery, and he asked me to join the two of you. I've never been up in a two-engine plane before. I suppose you have, Deidre?"

"I've been in my share of fixed-wing military transports, but nothing as luxurious as a private plane."

"I'm a little nervous about the whole thing, but excited too," Brigit said, twisting in her seat to see her daughter. In the rearview mirror, Nick noticed Deidre's expression soften slightly as she met her mother's glance. He took heart.

It would have been so much nicer to be sharing this moment alone with Deidre, but he didn't want to be selfish.

The image of Linc's letter—of his looping, at times unintelligible scrawl—leapt into his mind's eye. The letter had been heartbreaking in its simple, innocent plea. The letter had also worried Nick, as disorganized and childlike as the script had been. There was little doubt that Lincoln had loved Brigit Kavanaugh. He'd considered her the one and only true love of his life. He'd begged Nick to get to know Deidre better, to teach her about her legacy.

It had been Linc's insinuation that Deidre and he had an opportunity for a future together, one that had been denied to him and Brigit, that had truly alarmed him. Even if Linc had noticed his attraction to Deidre before he died, wasn't that an odd thing for him to suggest—that two strangers could share the future that the woman he loved and he couldn't?

Nick had been blown away when he'd read that part of Linc's letter. It underlined his worry that Linc hadn't been in his right mind when he changed the will. The man Nick had known since he was a boy would *never* have done something so impulsive, nor would he have made such naive assumptions about Deidre and him.

Nick had described to Deidre the carefree aspect of Linc's personality that surfaced at Christmastime, but Linc was typically not a whimsical man. Nick couldn't help but be worried that the change in Lincoln's will was more the result of a dying man's wish for a family than a rational, intelligent decision made with DuBois Enterprises and its thousands of employees in mind.

He couldn't tell Deidre that, though—couldn't show her Linc's letter. She'd jump to the conclusion it was *her* he doubted. He no longer even remotely suspected her of anything underhanded in her dealings with Lincoln. Deidre had truly been ignorant all this time of the identity of her sus-

pected natural father. She'd only had Lincoln's best interests
at heart once she'd met him.

He was certain of Deidre. But he was far from confident
that Deidre wouldn't equate his concern about the soundness
of Linc's decision-making at the end of his life with doubts
about her character. Worse, she might think that his concerns
about Lincoln's state of mind in regard to the will dimmed
Lincoln's faith that she was his daughter.

His ruminations were put on hold when they arrived at
the small airport. He showed Deidre and her mother onto his
Cessna and began his preflight check, glad to hear Deidre
and Brigit exchanging polite conversation about the changes
to the Harbor Town area. Deidre even laughed a time or two
as Brigit reminded her of several childhood moments.

The weather conditions were perfect. Nick took the plane
southward along the shoreline and then banked west, following the tip of a finger-shaped, sparkling Lake Michigan. The
tower had denied him permission to fly in too close to Chicago, but even several miles away they could see the clean,
sharp lines of the skyline as the Cessna glided over the brilliant blue lake.

"It looks like a fairy city," Deidre murmured from the
seat beside him.

He glanced at her. She gave him that little smile that always struck him like a fist to the gut. He exhaled with relief.

Apparently, he'd been forgiven for inviting Brigit without consulting her.

He knew what Deidre meant about Chicago. The tops
of the high rises were partially occluded by wispy clouds.
The city did look a little surreal, situated there on the distant shore.

"Do you ever miss it, Deidre?" Brigit asked from the seat
behind him. For a moment, Nick didn't understand what she
meant. Then he recalled that Deidre's permanent home had

been Chicago for all of her childhood. After the crash, Brigit had been forced to liquidate most of her and Derry's assets to pay legal damages to the Itani and Reyes families. She'd moved onto Sycamore Avenue, making the Harbor Town vacation house her permanent home.

"I miss it. I love Chicago. It's such a great city," Deidre replied.

"I understand you've visited Marc and Liam there several times over the past few years," Brigit said with what struck Nick as forced neutrality.

"Yes. I have," Deidre said.

An awkward silence ensued, and Nick thought he understood why. Deidre had never driven the short distance to Harbor Town to visit her mother when she was in the vicinity.

"Deidre, what was it like when you met Lincoln?" he heard Brigit ask after a moment. Her uncertain, timid voice struck him as highly uncharacteristic of the vibrant, intelligent older woman.

He waited, acutely aware of Deidre where she sat beside him even though he didn't watch her.

"Well…" Deidre began hesitantly, "the first time I saw him, Lincoln called me by your name, Mom."

"He did?" Brigit asked.

"Yes. My hair was long a few months back. I had just cut it off recently. It must have looked similar to when you were young and knew Lincoln," she explained in a rush. She cleared her throat. "You can see why he might have become confused momentarily, between me and your younger self. Oftentimes he was very sharp mentally, but other times… he'd drift."

Nick sensed her glance at him and briefly met her stare.

"When I explained to him I was Deidre, not Brigit Kavanaugh, he whispered, 'Deidre Jean' and he had this look on his face…almost as if he knew *precisely* who I was all of a sudden. That was one thing about Lincoln at the end of his life, don't you think, Nick?" she asked, looking to him for corroboration. "Sometimes, you'd think he was totally out of it and confused, and then suddenly he'd say something spot-on, and you got the impression he understood things even better than you did."

Nick nodded. "Sometimes it seemed like he didn't have a clue what I was talking about when it came to business decisions, and the next moment, he'd instruct me to do something completely brilliant that I hadn't thought of, and he'd have all the details and the names of the players perfectly intact in his memory."

Only the engines rang in his ears for the next few seconds, each of them seemingly lost in their thoughts.

"He must have recognized you on a very deep level," Brigit mused.

"He recognized you in me, Mom," Deidre said, her gaze out the front window.

"Maybe. But maybe he saw more than that."

The charged topic segued to more mundane matters. Nick found himself dwelling on Brigit's enigmatic statement, however, as they flew over the tiny, picturesque community of Harbor Town perched on the shore of the great lake.

What had Linc seen when he looked at Deidre? What had he seen when he saw Nick and her together? Nick was way too practical to think the answer was *a future,* which is what Linc had alluded to in his letter. Certainly Lincoln must have seen *something* though—something Deidre and he hadn't begun to envision, until recently, anyway.

Linc had craved a family for his entire life.

Who was Nick to argue at the possibility that Linc thought he recognized it standing right in front of him during the last days of his life?

* * *

Nick insisted on taking them out to an early dinner after the flight. Deidre found herself relaxing and enjoying herself as they dined at Bistro Campagne and Nick and Brigit told stories about Lincoln's favorite hobby, his horses. For the first time, Deidre discovered Lincoln had bred racehorses.

"Lincoln was well-known on the racing circuit. So was his father, George," Brigit assured Deidre when she expressed her amazement. "Lincoln owned Sacramento Sal, the winner of the Belmont Stakes and the Preakness two years running. Sal also placed at the Derby last year. Isn't that right, Nick?" Brigit asked. Nick nodded. Deidre caught her mother's eye. It struck her as bizarre that her mother followed horse racing all these years and knew so much about the topic.

"What is it, Deidre?" Brigit asked.

"Nothing," she murmured. "It's just that Nick took me out to McGraw Stables the other day. I had no idea you still rode. Addy McGraw told us you've been going out there since we bought the vacation home on Sycamore. I was surprised to learn from Lincoln that you were an excellent horsewoman. I'd had no idea until I met Addy you'd been riding all these years. Now I'm finding out you're an expert on racehorses, as well."

"Not an expert, by any means. I just read a few articles." Brigit's gaze sharpened on her. "Were you upset to find out I had ridden out at McGraw Stables, even when you were a child?"

Deidre's gaze flickered uncomfortably around the elegant dining room. "No. *Yes.* A little. Why didn't you ever take us to the stables?" she demanded.

"I expect you already know the reason for that," Brigit replied softly. "Do you think I wouldn't have adored doing it, sharing my love of horses with my children?"

Something pinched tight in her chest and throat. She

glanced at Nick uncertainly. He watched her with so much warmth in his eyes, she felt as if he was holding her...a silent, solid support.

"I feel like an outsider with the two of you when it comes to the topic of horses, that's all. I wouldn't know the front of a saddle from the back," Deidre said with a smile, not wanting the moment to turn morose.

"I told you—I've seen how horses respond to you," Nick said, stirring his iced tea idly. "Some people are just born with the ability to put animals at ease. I expect you're like that."

"I don't know what you mean," she said as the waiter cleared their plates. "All I did was pet a few horses while I was at The Pines."

"Captain was entranced by you," Nick murmured. His quiet voice sounded so warm, she glanced into his rugged face and was caught by the heat of his stare. "And Captain is no pushover—trust me. He's my horse."

She laughed. Nick shrugged and glanced at Brigit, unconcerned by her amusement. "She's not buying it. Maybe we'll just have to show her she's a natural."

"I expect you're right. Out of all my children, Deidre was always the animal lover, and they adored her in turn. I lost count of all the stray cats and dogs she brought home over the years, and that doesn't include the lame bird and wounded lizard she doctored on the back porch," Brigit said, smiling at Deidre.

After the meal, Nick pulled her aside in the dim, empty entryway of Bistro Campagne while Brigit used the ladies' room and made a quick phone call.

"I know you said we shouldn't do anything until we get the results of the paternity test, but I'd feel a lot more comfortable having Abel Warren contact you in regard to Lincoln's

will. He can advise you. I'll pay his fee. It's a fairly complicated document, and you could use someone in your corner."

Deidre studied her scarf as she tied it. "Actually…Marc
suggested someone he knows who specializes in estate law
take a look at it."

"Who did he recommend?" Nick asked.

Deidre swallowed and met his stare. What was he thinking? His cool, impassive professional expression was back in
place. She hesitated. "A man by the name of Mike Bonella."

Something shifted on his face.

"You know who he is?" Deidre asked.

"Yeah. He handled a case a few years back that was right
out of the pages of that old soap opera, *Dynasty*—the spoiled
children of Howard Ernst versus Howard's very young bride
of nine months. Bonella won. So did the young wife." His
eyebrows quirked up. "Sounds like your brother is looking
out for you."

Deidre closed her eyes briefly as mortification flashed
through her. "I haven't called him yet, Nick. I hope I don't
have to. Marc just gave me Bonella's name."

"I'm glad he gave it to you."

She started. "You are?"

Nick nodded. "The more sound advice you get, the better.
But Abel was loyal to the bone to Lincoln, and he'll be loyal
to you, in turn. He knows Lincoln's estate like no other. You
can trust him. It wouldn't hurt to at least talk to Abel and get
his insight on the whole thing. I can tell you what I know,
but because of the circumstances, there are those who would
think the information I give you is skewed to my benefit. I'd
rather you didn't have to worry about that."

Dread settled like lead in the pit of her stomach. She
wasn't sure how she was supposed to feel about Nick thinking it was a good idea to have so many legal guns on her side.

"Why would you recommend I have someone in my corner? Have you decided to contest the will?"

"No. I know now you didn't have any part in coercing Lincoln in any way. I'm just saying you should get good legal counsel because I don't want anyone making ugly accusations about me influencing you unduly. If you want access to your funds before we get the results of the paternity test, just tell Abel. You are free to do that now, Deidre. I wouldn't stop you."

Heat warmed her cheeks. Talk about an awkward situation.

"I told you—I don't want to do anything like that until I get the official word as to whether or not I'm Lincoln's child. If I took any money without knowing that, if I did *anything* without knowing that first, I'd feel like a…"

"What?"

"Fraud," she whispered.

He frowned and glanced toward the hallway behind them. Deidre turned to see her mother approaching, a smile on her face. The loaded conversation with Nick would just have to wait.

After they'd dropped her mother off on Sycamore Avenue, Deidre asked if they could stop at the Shop and Save. They were getting out of the car when Nick got a call.

"I should take this," he said, glancing up from his phone. "Do you mind if I just stay in the car?"

"No, of course not," Deidre assured.

By the time she returned, he was still on the call. He hung up and got out of the car, but she'd already tossed the two light bags into the backseat.

"Is that all you got?" he asked as they got back in the sedan.

"It's just dessert. I thought we might want something

later," she explained as she put on her seat belt. "What?" she asked when she saw his frown.

"I have to fly to San Francisco for a few days. There was a chemical fire at one of our pharmaceutical companies."

"Was anyone hurt?"

"One man has been hospitalized with significant burns, but he's stable," he said as he drove through the parking lot. "All the other employees were treated for minor injuries at the local emergency room and discharged. I'm thankful no one was killed. The fire was extensive though.

"I'm sorry about having to leave," he told her when he pulled into the driveway a few minutes later and put the car into park. "I make it a habit to go and inspect our facilities immediately following accidents. I don't like to hear things second- and thirdhand about something so crucial."

She swallowed, struck by the way he kept saying "our."

"There's nothing to be sorry for," she assured him. "You're absolutely right. Please—go and do whatever is necessary to make sure everyone there is safe."

He glanced into the backseat. "Come on. I'll help you with the bags."

"No," she insisted. "There are just a couple items. You have more important things to think about."

He frowned. "You're important."

She smiled. "Well, I'm not going anywhere."

He gave a quick bark of laughter. "Good," he said. "Because I'll be back to Harbor Town before you know it." He leaned over and kissed her.

A minute later, she got out of the car with her bags in tow and waved as he backed out of the drive. She trudged up the squeaking, frozen front stairs to the dark cottage. Nick's goodbye kisses were always delicious, but they only seemed to highlight the empty, heavy feeling that inevitably settled in her belly when he was gone.

Chapter Nine

Deidre spent the following morning at the Family Center helping Colleen paint a new playroom for clients' children. It was the perfect opportunity for Colleen to pump Deidre about information in regard to her date with Nick and the outing with their mother. She'd forgotten to mention Addy's comments about Brigit to Colleen. Colleen was just as stunned as Deidre had been to learn their mother had been horseback riding in secret all this time.

"Liam was right," Colleen said as she rolled bright yellow paint onto the wall. "Mom has been eaten away by guilt all these years. She wanted to keep Lincoln and her love of horses and that part of her life...*all* of it separate from us."

Deidre said nothing, just resumed doing some corner work with a brush. Unfortunately, the "all of it" that Brigit had kept separate from Deidre was half of her family.

That afternoon, she purchased a box of assorted cookies from Celino's and drove it out to the McGraw Stables.

Addy gave her a huge toothy grin and a hug for her gift. She sat with the friendly woman for a half hour at her kitchen table, sipping coffee and listening to Addy reminisce about her mother.

It struck Deidre how strange it was, the different faces an individual showed the people in their life. Addy found Brigit Kavanaugh to be an unfailingly kind, courageous, talented horsewoman, and a loyal friend. Derry had always respected his wife's strength of character and her role as a mother. As an adult looking back in time, Deidre realized Derry had certainly found Brigit attractive…alluring. Her mother had a certain elusive quality about her, as though part of her would always remain a mystery. Lincoln, too, had been captivated by Brigit, idealizing her, putting her up on a pedestal, never entirely getting over his love for her.

As a child, Deidre had lived in the secure cocoon of her mother's warmth and love, never doubting it would be there any more than she doubted air would enter her lungs on her next inhale. When she'd learned what Brigit had done, it'd been like having the breath knocked clean out of her.

"Your mama is a great lady," Addy concluded fondly, drawing Deidre out of her reflections. "All that charity work she does, and she visits a lot of the older ladies in town, people in need, cheering them up, taking them to their doctor's appointments and such. They don't make them like your mother anymore."

Deidre smiled and patted Addy's weathered hand. "Thank you for talking with me about my mom."

Addy's expression softened. "You come out here anytime to talk about anything you like, you hear?"

Deidre returned to Cedar Cottage, feeling thoughtful. She wrapped Christmas presents and placed them under the tree, admiring the way the colored lights struck the festive paper.

The sound of ringing jarred her. For a few seconds, she

just stared at her cell phone. What if this was it—the call from GenLabs she'd been both dreading and anticipating for weeks on end?

She took courage and glanced at the number. She exhaled in relief.

"Hi," she said, smiling as sat back on the cushions.

"Hi. What are you up to?" Nick asked, his deep, quiet voice causing a thrill of awareness to go through her.

"Really important stuff—wrapping Christmas presents and staring at the Christmas tree. How are things there?"

"As good as can be expected," Nick replied evenly enough, but she heard the grim edge to his tone. "We inspected the plant this morning and I met with the safety director and manager."

"How is the man who was injured?"

"His name's Edgar Grant. He's obviously not the most comfortable with third degree burns on his legs and hip, but he'll be out of the hospital in a few days. His sense of humor is intact, anyway."

"Did you actually visit him in the hospital?" Deidre asked.

"Yeah, just briefly. The nurse was about to dress his burns. What else did you do today?"

She'd been about to express her amazement that the CEO of an enormous conglomerate had taken the time to visit an injured employee of a small subsidiary plant but she ceased when he changed the topic. Nick obviously didn't think his actions were noteworthy, even if she did. "Oh, I helped Colleen paint a playroom at the Family Center and I took some cookies out to Addy McGraw. Addy talked a lot about my mom."

"She's a real fan of your mom, that's for sure." He paused. "I hope it's okay for me to say, but I like your mother, too. She reminds me a little of Lily DuBois."

"Really?" Deidre asked, taken aback.

"Not in looks, but in manner. She's a sharp, classy lady. I can see why Linc was so taken with her for all those years. You haven't really had the opportunity to let me have it for asking her to go up in the plane with us, by the way," he added. Deidre could perfectly picture the half amused, half wary tilt of his mouth.

"You're lucky. The outing went so well, I lost the urge."

"Really?"

She sighed and lay on her back on the couch. "Really," she said, hearing all of the doubt, hurt and hope she felt in regard to her mother infused into the one word.

A pregnant pause ensued. Even though neither of them spoke, Deidre felt strangely connected to Nick in that moment, despite the thousands of miles that separated them. She had a sudden, vivid image of him sitting in a chair with his back to a desk and facing a floor-to-ceiling window. His tie was loosened and his hair had fallen onto his forehead. She doubted it was anything but her imagination, but her heart throbbed in her breast as if she'd truly seen him.

"Life sure can be crazy at times," he murmured, his voice sounding so close he might have been right next to her.

"Yeah...but it can be nice, too," she replied quietly.

"Deidre..."

"Hmm?"

"Maybe I liked your mother because she looked so much like you."

She smiled. She had the distinct impression that wasn't what he'd planned to say just seconds before. "I think it's the other way around. I look like her."

"Either way, my point is the same."

She chuckled and turned on her side, drawing up her knees. She felt lulled and content, lying there and listening to the sound of Nick's low, gruff voice in her ear.

"Where are you at?" she asked.

"At the San Francisco office. I thought I'd get a little work done while I was here. I miss you."

Deidre blinked in amazement at the unexpected declaration. "I miss you, too."

She heard a rustle and the sound of his chair squeaking. "I better go. I'll be back in Harbor Town the day after tomorrow."

"Okay. Nick?"

"Yeah?"

"Sleep well," she said feelingly.

There was a stretched pause. "You, too."

Nick hit the disconnect button on his phone and set it on the desk.

"I didn't hear you knock," he said, leveling a stare at John Kellerman, DuBois Enterprises's chief legal officer. He stood several feet in front of Nick's desk. John was a formidable figure with iron-gray hair and an unparalleled knowledge of corporate law.

"I just came in to have a word with you. I knocked but you were obviously too wrapped up in your conversation to notice."

Nick didn't reply. He sincerely doubted John had knocked. He'd overheard Nick talking to Deidre. Nick waited patiently in order to see the direction of John's attack. John suddenly smiled and shook his head.

"There must be some explanation. I know you too well to think this anything other than brilliant maneuvering. You know precisely what you're doing, I suppose, sleeping with the enemy?" he asked with a bark of mirthless laughter, waving at Nick's cell phone. "Not that I'm arguing with your choice—she's a tasty one, there's never been any argument in that direction."

"Shut up, John."

John flinched back at his quiet words.

"You're playing too close to the flame, Nick. I understand getting closer to Deidre Kavanaugh will only help you to manipulate this nightmare of a situation with Lincoln's will, but be careful of getting burned. We only have to look at Lincoln as evidence for the fact that Deidre has the power to thoroughly befuddle a man."

"Speaking of someone flying dangerously close to the flame," Nick said, his voice cold.

John's expression flattened at Nick's obvious warning that he was treading too close to personal territory. "I see," he said stiffly. "You're telling me that you can handle this on your own. I suppose you're right. I have every reason to trust your opinion on how to get things done. You've never failed DuBois Enterprises before."

Nick watched silently as John sat down in the one of the leather chairs in front of his desk.

"At least I can say one thing for you, Nick—you're willing to go to any extreme to make sure our interests are protected. I think it's time we start to firm up our plan of action if we should receive the news from GenLabs that Deidre Kavanaugh is, indeed, Lincoln DuBois's biological child, don't you?" John asked.

The next morning, Deidre did some shopping and unloaded the groceries at Cedar Cottage, watered the plants at Liam and Natalie's house and met Colleen for lunch. Afterward, she went over to the Harbor Town Public Library and found some references on DuBois Enterprises infrastructure and product lines. She read for three and a half hours straight before her back started to ache. She returned the material to the librarian, amazed to realize she'd barely scratched the surface in regard to learning about the company.

By the time she returned home, the sun was dipping into a

frigid-looking Lake Michigan and Cedar Cottage was draped in shadow. Her fingers felt chilled once she'd removed her coat. Without turning on any lights, she went into the living room and turned on the gas fireplace, warming her hands. She went completely still when she heard a door squeak down the hallway.

Someone is in the house.

She spun around in alarm, only to see a tall shadow enter the living room. For a few seconds, she just stared, sure she must be dreaming.

"Deidre?"

"Nick?" she managed in a thin, amazed whisper.

He came closer, the light from the flames making his familiar features resolve out of shadow. "I'm sorry. I didn't mean to scare you. I just got here before you did. I was just checking to make sure you weren't around. Your car wasn't here, but the front door was unlocked."

"It was?" she whispered. She'd inserted her key and twisted when she'd entered just now, not noticing the lock hadn't been fastened. Nick stepped closer. She stood transfixed, studying every nuance of his face as if she hadn't seen him in years. His expression was sober and tense. "I must have left it unlocked when I brought the groceries home earlier. What are you doing here? Is something wrong?"

"Yeah," he said gruffly, stepping toward her.

"What?" she asked in confusion and rising alarm, only recognizing the telltale heat in his eyes after he grasped her shoulders and drew her against him. "Nick—"

He silenced her with his mouth.

He kissed her, a little rough…a lot sweet.

His taste had a drugging effect on her senses. His hands moved over her shoulders and down her sides, cupping her breasts in his palms before he wrapped his hands gently around her ribs, rubbing her back muscles with his fingertips. He leaned over her, deepening their already voracious kiss. His grasp lowered onto her hips, where he massaged her flesh hungrily. Deidre had the strangest impression he was detailing the sensation of her just like she'd been hungrily searching his features just moments ago, wondrous at his presence.

She pressed tighter against him, seeking his male heat. He groaned in sudden dissatisfaction and lifted her so that their mouths, bellies and groins sealed tight. Deidre wrapped her legs around his hips. He rocked her against him, her softness against his hardness.

She groaned roughly at the same moment desire clenched tight at her core.

The next thing she knew, she was falling against the couch cushions. Nick came down over her, straddling her hips. She watched his rigid features cast in firelight as he rapidly unfastened her blouse and opened it. He stroked along the sides of her waist and ribs. She once again had the impression it wasn't a casual touch, but that he was absorbing the very sensation of her. Her eyes moistened and she blinked, wanting to see him clearly in that electrical moment. He slid his fingers beneath the front clasp of her bra and gave his wrist a flick. He peeled the cups off her skin.

A stab of thwarted desire went through her when instead of touching her breasts, he began to unfasten her jeans with quick, nimble fingers. His gaze remained fixed where she wanted him to caress, however, making her nipples tighten. He drew her jeans and panties off her, then unfastened and lowered his own pants.

His eyelids squeezed tight and his nostrils flared when he was fully sheathed inside her. Deidre felt so full of him in that moment; she was inundated…possessed. She murmured his name between pants for air and he opened his eyes. They seemed to glow silver in the firelight as he stared down at her.

"Another emergency came up," he said.

"What?"

"I had to see you. At all costs," he grated out between a clenched jaw. He withdrew and sunk back into her. Deidre gasped and furrowed her fingers into his hair. It was hard to form words with him pulsing high and hard inside of her.

She drew him down toward her mouth and managed in a whisper, "I'm so glad you did."

A while later, Nick lay with his weight partially on Deidre and partially on the couch. Both of them gasped for air, their muscles limp in the aftermath of a lightning strike of passion and need.

"What's so funny?" Nick wondered, lifting his head to see her face when he heard her soft laughter.

"You're still wearing your coat," Deidre said.

He gave a grunt of amusement and shucked off the coat, tossing it over the back of the couch. He let his forehead drop to the cushion again. "You just now noticed?"

She nuzzled his chin and he turned toward her, their lips a mere inch apart. "I didn't see anything but you."

He didn't say anything, but she saw his eyes glint in the firelight. His mouth settled on hers, and there was more than just the residue of passion in his kiss.

"Welcome back to Harbor Town," she murmured a moment later, brushing her lips against his as she spoke.

"With a welcome like that, I might never leave."

"With a hello like that, I might never let you," she assured, before she pressed her lips against his small grin.

Deidre was still smiling an hour later when she heard the shower shut off in the bathroom. She started the sauce for the beef filets she'd already prepared. By the time Nick walked into the kitchen a few minutes later, she was pouring it over the beef.

"What's this?" Nick asked.

She glanced back and did a double take. He looked extremely good. His hair was still damp. He wore jeans and the dark blue cotton tee he'd had on beneath his button-down shirt. The short sleeves highlighted his strong-looking forearms and muscular biceps. She caught a subtle whiff of his shower-clean skin and had an urge to bury her nose in it. He was staring at the table she'd set for two.

"It's dinner, what do you think?" she said, laughing as she set down their plates. She lit the two candles she'd placed on the table.

He was there when she turned around. He leaned down and kissed her. Deidre closed her hands around the dense muscle of his upper arms and savored the scent and texture of him.

"Thanks. It smells great. I didn't know you could cook," Nick said as they both sat. "What other secrets are you keeping?"

"You should taste it before you draw any conclusions," she said, stabbing her fork into an apple-and-walnut spinach salad. "I like to cook, but didn't get much of an opportunity while I was in the army. I haven't tried this peppercorn filet recipe in ages, so eat it at your own risk."

Nick took a bite of his filet. "It's *fantastic*," he muttered after a moment. "Apparently the army hasn't dulled your cooking instincts."

"I'm just glad eating army food hasn't completely killed my taste buds," Deidre said, watching him with a smile as he ate another bite of beef with flattering haste.

When they'd finished and were sipping their decaf, Nick suddenly stood and walked over to where his coat was hung on the coat tree. He withdrew what looked like a black velvet pouch from his coat pocket.

He sat down again and placed the large pouch on the table.

"This is for you. I stopped at The Pines on my way back to Harbor Town and picked it up."

"What is it?" Deidre asked, eyeing the pouch.

"It's something Linc asked me to give you in his letter," Nick replied gruffly. She met his stare. He frowned. "I'm sorry for not giving it to you until now."

Deidre loosened the drawstring on the bag. She reached inside and withdrew a smaller pouch.

"I took everything out of their storage boxes and put them in these bags for easier transport," Nick explained as she poked her fingers into the small pouch.

Deidre gasped.

"It's gorgeous," she whispered, gaping wide-eyed at an exquisite diamond and sapphire pavé ring. Something occurred to her and she twitched her hand beneath the larger velvet bag, feeling numerous hard items within. The pouch was *filled* with jewelry.

"I can't accept any of this," she said, stunned.

Nick grasped her wrist when she went to set the pouch and ring on the table.

"Yes, you can. Linc left it to you as a separate request in the letter. This jewelry used to belong to Lily DuBois. These were her finest pieces. There were several other pieces that were left to the entire estate, but Linc handpicked these items for you to have exclusively. They were locked in a safe at The Pines."

Deidre stared at him in amazement. He released her wrist. After a pause, she once again picked up the bag. She set all of the smaller pouches in her lap and smoothed the larger velvet bag onto the table. Nick said nothing, just watched, as she withdrew all of the separate pieces. By the time she'd finished, a breathtaking display lay on the black velvet— a sapphire and diamond set, including necklace, earrings and ring; a stunning pair of diamond earrings and matching wreath necklace; a pair of sunflower earrings that included large center diamond studs and a matching necklace with row after row of large, sparkling diamonds; a ruby, diamond and platinum set that included a flower motif with the ruby as the center and diamonds forming the petals and leaves; and, lastly, a diamond and platinum brooch of a horse in midstride. The artistry of the items was unlike anything Deidre had ever laid eyes on—exquisite in detail, unapologetically lush but delicate at once, luxurious without being ostentatious. Deidre ran her fingers over the running horse in wonder.

"George had that brooch made for Lily when Gallant Hunter, one of their horses, was inducted into the National Museum of Racing's Hall of Fame."

She glanced up at Nick mutely.

"I apologize again for not bringing them when I first came to Harbor Town," he said quietly.

"I understand why you didn't," she whispered. "You shouldn't have brought them now. Maybe after we hear about the genetic testing, but—"

"They're yours, whatever happens," Nick said gruffly. "It's one of the few specific bequests Linc made. I've thought about it, and he would want you to have these things no matter what the outcome of the testing. I'm convinced of that."

She shook her head, overwhelmed by emotion, and began to put away the priceless jewelry. "Take it," she entreated when she'd replaced all the items in the bag.

"They're yours, Deidre."

She swallowed with difficulty, but it didn't work. She felt choked with emotion. "I don't know what's mine and what's not anymore."

He assessed her soberly. "What do you mean by that?"

She shook her head and stared out the window blankly. She was having difficulty meeting his eyes for some reason. Was it guilt?

"I'm not so sure anymore that I deserve anything from Lincoln. He didn't even know me, not really. It was *you* he knew and loved for a lifetime."

"There's no official timetable on love. Lincoln believed you were his."

She narrowed her gaze on him. "Do you believe that, Nick?"

He inhaled slowly. Was he striving for caution in his answer? Deidre wondered. "Belief isn't as important to me as it is to you in these circumstances. I know that *Lincoln* believed."

"I wish I knew what to believe," she said, giving Nick a desperate glance. "I'm so happy Lincoln had faith that I was his child. I want *so* much to be Lincoln's biological daughter. But every time I imagine it being true, I feel so sad and mad because he's gone. Derry's gone. I'm right back where I started, without a father."

"I'm not so sure about that. You have a mother, Deidre."

She met his stare, remorse spiking through her. "You must think I sound so ungrateful."

"No, I don't think that." He frowned and sat back in his chair. Deidre had the distinct impression he was torn about whether to go on about the subject.

"What is it, Nick?" Deidre asked. "Do you think I've been too hard on my mother?"

"I understand you're mad about being kept in the dark all these years, missing out on a relationship with Lincoln. But your mom lost her husband and she lost her best friend. She lost you for a good portion of her life and probably fears she'll never get you back. I can't help but feeling bad for her." He shook his head and gave a sheepish wave. "I know—it's none of my business."

"I don't think that it's none of your business. I'm just confused as to why you care one way or another," she said.

"You've been urging Mom and me to resolve our differences. Why?"

For a few seconds he didn't reply. "I guess I just worry about you."

"*Me?* You want to make sure I have a mommy to look out for me? I've been taking care of myself for a long, long time, Nick," she said, chuckling.

"I don't like the idea of you being alone in the future."

Her mirth faded. Was he telling her he was trying to prepare her for the fact that what was between them wasn't permanent? Was he implying that she needed to build up her support because there was a good chance she would be cast adrift again sometime in the near future?

She closed her mouth and cleared her throat. Of course that's not what he meant. Hadn't he been the definition of a passionate, interested male in the past week? She was just being paranoid.

"You don't have to worry about me. Or my mother."

"You've told me the story about Brigit. I feel for her, that's all. She finds out her husband has had an affair. She's devastated…hurting. She flees West and finds comfort from an old friend."

"It was selfish of her. Pure and simple. There were much better ways to handle the situation with Dad than to get him back by having her own affair," Deidre insisted, her jaw tilted up defiantly.

Nick's eyes flashed. "Do you know for a fact Brigit was intent on payback? You loved Lincoln after knowing him only for months…weeks…days, maybe? He was a wonderful man. Wouldn't you consider running to him, after a betrayal like your mother experienced? Imagine how deep your mother's feelings must have been for him, given their long history. Maybe it was a mistake for them to sleep together, but you don't have to twist your mom into the wicked witch.

I won't argue that Brigit made a huge mistake. She's paid a heavy toll for it. Don't you think she's suffered enough?"

Deidre just stared at him, amazed that he saw the topic so differently than her. As an outsider, did he perhaps see it more clearly? Was her perspective hazed by a teenager's pain and simplistic view of the adult world?

"Look, I'm sorry for bringing it up," he mumbled. "I'm sorry, period. I don't want to fight with you. I just wanted to give you the jewelry. I don't know how the hell we got here."

She stared at the velvet pouch, longing and doubt warring inside her.

"To whom would that jewelry belong if not you?" Nick asked after a grave pause.

She met his stare. "You," she mouthed.

He nodded slowly and leaned toward her. "So no matter what happens, it's yours," he said before he kissed her trembling lips.

Deidre stared out the kitchen window the next morning, watching a gentle snowfall. Nick and she had gone to the Starling Hotel last night and had Lily DuBois's precious jewels locked in the hotel safe. This morning, however, Deidre felt as if she carried a priceless treasure in her heart. Her entire world sparkled.

"Hey."

She turned and smiled at the source of her newfound joy. "Hey."

"You ready to go?" Nick murmured, stepping toward her and wrapping his hands around her shoulders.

"Yes," she replied, turning her face up to receive his kiss.

"Do horses like the snow?" she asked after a moment.

"It depends on the horse," Nick said wryly next to her mouth before he kissed her again. He grabbed her hand. "Come on, I told your mother we'd pick her up by ten."

Nervousness fluttered in her belly as they approached Sycamore Avenue, but Brigit was walking out of the house at the same moment Nick pulled into the driveway. She walked toward them through a gentle snow wearing a pair of riding breeches, supple brown leather boots and a dark green anorak. Brigit gave her a warm smile through the windshield as she walked to the car. Gratitude swelled in Deidre's breast at the knowledge that her mother had understood she wasn't quite ready to go into the house.

"It's a wonderful day for a ride," Brigit enthused as she got in the backseat. Deidre glanced back at her mother. Brigit beamed at her. Was Deidre's happiness with the world contagious? Her mother seemed to glow with health and good spirits.

"I'm so excited. To think—I'm finally going to teach one of my children to ride."

Deidre returned her smile. "If I don't fall off and break my neck," she said under her breath as she turned in her seat.

"With teachers like Nick and I?" Brigit asked jovially. "Not a chance."

As it turned out, Deidre had more than Nick and her mother for teachers. A half an hour later, she sat on the back of a brown mare named Grace as she was taught to find her seat. Nick held the horse steady while Addy adjusted one stirrup, Brigit adjusted the other and Evan, Addy's husband, silently oversaw their progress. Deidre held the reins and tried to get used to the unusual sensation of sitting on a large animal's back.

"Don't jam your foot so tight in the stirrup," Addy instructed.

"Keep your posture straight, but try to relax," Brigit added.

"Quit poking at the girl and put her out on the lunge," Evan chimed in.

"The lunge?" Deidre asked nervously. She petted Grace's neck soothingly when Nick let go and her hooves shifted. Was she transferring her anxiety to the animal?

"It's easiest to teach you how to post on a lunge line," Nick explained as he attached a leather strap to Grace's bridle.

"And what's posting again?" Deidre wondered uncertainly.

"A horse's trot is bouncy," Nick explained. "Posting helps to smooth out the jarring motion. You rise in the saddle for every other stride. Can you show her while I explain?" Nick asked Brigit.

Brigit nodded. Evan brought her a sleek-looking, near-black horse that had already been saddled. Deidre watched in admiration as her mother mounted with ease and an elegant poise. She straightened her spine, trying to model her mother's perfect posture. She watched Brigit urge the horse to a trot within the fenced enclosure.

"See how she rides the trot?" Nick said. Deidre listened intently as he described the necessary motion for the post, watching her mother with a tight focus, trying to memorize the movement.

"Are you ready to try it?" Nick asked.

"Not really," Deidre said doubtfully. Her mom had made it seem like the easiest thing on earth to post on a horse, but she was quite sure it wasn't.

"It'll be okay," Nick assured her. "You'll circle me while I have Grace on the line. It'll give you a chance to learn to post without having to worry about guiding her."

"Can I lunge her?" Brigit asked breathlessly as she dismounted and handed her reins to Evan.

Nick glanced at Deidre, his eyebrows quirked upward. She gave him a shaky, hopeful smile.

"Sure," he murmured, handing the lunge line to Brigit.

It took Deidre several minutes to get the required motion as she jostled around for a while on Grace's back, circling the enclosure. After concentrating and shifting her muscles into the new movement, things seemed to smooth. She heard a shout from Addy and glanced through the gentle snowfall toward the fence.

"You've got it!" Addy called.

A surge of excitement went through her as she matched the rhythm of her body to that of the horse. It felt exhilarating.

She grinned and glanced at her mother. Brigit's expression as she held the lunge line was beyond proud.

Chapter Ten

"That was so much fun!" Deidre called back to Nick two hours later as they approached the stables at a slow trot, Brigit riding several yards in front of them. White Christmas lights twinkled against the gray winter sky from the trees that lined the McGraw Stables entry drive. It'd been indescribable, practicing with Nick and her mother on one of the many well-cleared paths and finally taking her first full all-out ride, independent of the lunge line or instruction.

Riding a horse felt similar to soaring free on a high dive. It was a heart-pounding, thrilling…quite possibly addictive experience.

She glanced back, grinning, only to see Nick watching her, just a hint of a smile tilting his firm mouth. Her heart surged in her breast. Snowflakes dusted his dark hair and jacket. She'd seen him riding a few times at The Pines. While her mother reminded her of an elegant equestrian princess, Nick rode like he was one with the animal.

"I suppose you're happy," she said quietly as he came alongside her. "You guessed I'd love it, and you were right."

He gave a small shrug and spoke quietly enough for only her to hear. "I wasn't being smug," he corrected. "I was just appreciating the rear view."

Deidre snorted softly with laughter and brought Grace to a halt, thrilling at the manner in which the animal followed her slightest prompt. She was riding the high from her horseback ride until Nick helped her dismount. He noticed her grimace.

"You'll be a little sore until you get more used to it," he said, hiding his smile as Deidre rubbed her hip and bottom.

"It won't take her long to get a thicker hide," Addy said mirthfully as she and Evan joined them and took the horses' reins.

Brigit laughed. "Don't worry. I'll give you a priceless bath soak that will help things considerably."

"You'd better or I might never walk again, let alone ride a horse," Deidre said as she took a step and groaned. She took her mother's hand instinctively when it was offered. "I don't recall getting this sore when you taught me how to ride a bike."

"Everything gets tougher when we get older," Brigit said, grinning.

Deidre smiled and walked alongside her mom. She wondered where Nick was and glanced back. He stood watching the two of them, a subtle but unmistakable expression of satisfaction on his face. She held out her free hand to him and he came alongside her to take it. Brigit noticed the gesture and took on a satisfied expression herself.

Deidre didn't mind their apparent watching over her. For the first time in a long time she felt at peace with herself and the world.

"What are you doing for Christmas Eve, Nick?" Brigit asked as they strolled toward the farmhouse.

Nick's gray eyes flickered over Deidre. "I can't say that I have any set plans," he said neutrally.

Brigit paused in the drive. Since Deidre held hands with both Nick and her mother, they came to a halt along with her.

"Christmas is only a few days away. Won't you two please come to my house to celebrate?" Brigit entreated earnestly.

Deidre glanced at Nick, but he was studying her for a reaction. A movement caught her attention out of the corner of her eye. She glanced toward the farmhouse. There was a dark blue car parked on the drive that hadn't been there when they left for their ride. A man was standing next to the open driver's side door holding a telephoto camera up to his face.

"Get out of here," Nick barked so abruptly that it startled Deidre. He broke his hold and took several aggressive steps forward.

The man immediately ducked back into the car, slammed the door and whipped the car around in the turnabout. He drove rapidly down the drive toward the rural route.

"Who was that?" Brigit asked, bewildered.

"Photographer." He looked at Deidre grimly. "Either someone tipped off the press about me being here in Harbor Town or someone has leaked the story about you and Lincoln's will."

Deidre was initially more amazed than anything else that someone would want to sneak photos of Nick or her. Who cared about *her* life? Nick's life was more understandable, but still…why had he reacted so intently?

When she fully took in Nick's grim profile as he drove them back to town, some of the seriousness of the situation started to settle. Things felt even weightier when she saw Nick checking his rearview mirror.

Was he actually worried they were being followed?

What if this were the beginning of a media frenzy? She dreaded the idea of the press making insulting insinuations about herself, her mother, Derry, Lincoln or Nick, and what if they began to turn their focus onto Marc and his campaign?

"What are you most worried will happen if the press knows about the will?" she asked Nick privately as they drove to Cedar Cottage.

"I'm not so much worried about what will happen. I'm worried about who leaked the story and why," he said.

"Aren't you coming in?" Deidre asked when Nick didn't shut off the engine once he'd pulled up next to Cedar Cottage.

"I should go back to the hotel and see if we can't contain things if there has been a leak. I'll need to speak with Carrie Sharr, our pubic relations officer, and come up with some kind of official position in regard to Lincoln's will."

"Official position?" Deidre asked weakly.

He looked at her somberly. "It's not a big deal, Deidre. We would have had to do it soon, anyway. I just wasn't expecting the press to get ahold of this so quickly. Do me a favor and don't leave the cottage for a few hours until I get back."

Her mouth fell open in surprise. "Is it that serious that I have to hide behind closed doors?"

He shook his head. He removed his glove and touched her jaw. "I'm just being cautious."

"All right," Deidre agreed.

He nodded once and put his hand back in his glove.

She returned to the cottage, closed and double locked the door. She'd never once considered since finding out about Lincoln's will that there might come a time when her privacy was compromised. The realization struck her as unsettling…even sinister somehow. She'd spent her whole life taking her anonymity for granted. Now, perhaps all of that was going to change.

She tried to shake off her oppressive mood. She lit the Christmas tree and took a hot bath to soothe her sore muscles. Afterward, she turned on the radio and set out the ingredients to bake some cookies. She was in the process of spooning dough onto a cookie sheet when she heard a knock. She wiped off her hands and headed toward the door, pausing as she reached out to open it. What if it wasn't Nick?

She kept the chain lock hooked and opened the door only a few inches, peering cautiously into the crevice.

"John," she muttered in shock when she saw John Kellerman standing on her front porch.

"Hello, Deidre. I thought it was high time you and I had a talk."

A few minutes later Deidre placed a cup of coffee in front of John Kellerman and sat down at the table warily. His distinguished appearance and elegant suit made her feel like she was attending a business meeting instead of sitting in a cozy kitchen wearing yoga pants and a T-shirt, the delicious scent of sugar cookies beginning to permeate the air.

"What can I do for you, John?"

"I just thought it was important for us to meet, that's all. You have been named as the co-owner of the company. I'm not the only executive officer who'd like to meet with you."

"I'll bet," Deidre muttered under her breath. Her gaze flickered up to meet his. "So everyone at DuBois knows about Lincoln's new will?" she asked, thinking about the photographer today and Nick's concern about a news leak.

"Only the top officers—a mere handful of people."

"I see," Deidre said, although she wasn't so sure she did. Nick hadn't mentioned anything about telling the top people at DuBois about Lincoln's will, or Deidre or where they might find her. She'd known he'd told John, of course, but that's all. She supposed she shouldn't be surprised. If John was in on things, it made sense that the other top executives were, as well. "I was under the impression that things were sort of on hold until I heard about the genetic testing."

John nodded and took a sip of his coffee. "Yes, that piece of information is crucial, of course. And it's silly for us to plan any future contingencies until we have it in hand."

Deidre's spine stiffened. She didn't care for his haughty coldness. *"We?"* she emphasized. The way he'd answered her question gave her the distinct, unsettling impression that the "we" John referred to were the DuBois executives. "I thought that whatever happens after we get the test results was exclusively up to Nick. He was the one whose shares were diminished in the new will. *He* was the previous sole heir."

"That's right," John agreed, nodding his head. "If the testing comes back negative in regard to paternity, there's a clear course of action, of course. Lincoln will have changed his will on mistaken information that you were his biological daughter. If the testing proves Lincoln *was* your father... well." John gave a small, polite smile that struck Deidre as fake. "I assume Nick is being honest with you about the fact that he's unsure precisely what he'll do if the results come back positive."

"He's been honest with me," Deidre said. A chill skittered down her spine. Her hands and feet suddenly felt cold.

John gave her a confidential nod. "I understand from him that you two have grown close. It's good to hear he's been up front with you about his concerns in regard to Lincoln's letter."

She started to question him but paused. Did she really want to hear whatever this stranger had to say?

"I don't blame Nick, of course. It's very troubling, that letter," John mused.

"You've seen it?" Deidre asked hollowly. She recalled how she'd asked to see Lincoln's last letter to Nick and how Nick had refused her.

I have my reasons for saying no, Deidre. Don't take offense.

"Oh, yes. Of course I've seen the letter. It's a very important piece of evidence when this case—" He paused suddenly and gave her an apologetic nod. "*If* this case should go to trial. That letter makes it clear Lincoln wasn't entirely in his right mind at the time he changed the will and declared you and Nick coheirs."

"Really?" she asked. The coldness had now reached her heart.

John shrugged dispassionately. "I knew Lincoln for thirty-one years. He was an astonishingly acute business leader. That letter he gave Nick is clearly the incoherent ramblings of someone with an organic dementia. No one—least of all a court of law—will consider his disorganized pleas to Nick as anything but the product of a sad, sick man."

"And...and Nick agrees with you about this?"

John blinked at her question. "Agrees?" he asked blankly. "Nick is the one who originally expressed those concerns to me when he showed me the letter. He was incredulous that Lincoln could do something so impulsive and naive." John leaned closer, examining her expression. "I thought Nick had showed you the letter. He hasn't?"

Deidre shook her head.

John looked patently uncomfortable. "I'm sorry, I'd only assumed..." He glanced at her, hesitating. "You *do* understand that if it can be proven in court that Lincoln was of unsound mind, it will negate the will where he named you as coheir? The old will—the one where Nick is the sole heir—will become solvent again."

Deidre felt the blood rush out of her head. She seemed to be seeing John Kellerman through a haze. She tried to troll through her memories in regard to what Nick had told her in regard to contesting the will, but it was difficult with John staring at her like a hawk. Besides, Nick had told her those things before they'd began to trust each other, before they'd become involved…

…before Deidre had fallen in love with him.

It felt like the invisible hand gripping at her heart transferred to her throat.

"Yes, Nick told me as much…I think so…" she muttered hoarsely, hazily recalling some of the things Nick had said in the car on those first nights he'd come to Harbor Town.

This time, John's relieved expression did strike her as contrived. "Good. I know Nick too well to believe he'd ever do anything underhanded when it came to his…*association* with you," the older man said delicately.

Deidre went still. She searched John's face, quite sure she was being paranoid. "Nick told you that he and I are involved?" she asked, her voice near a whisper.

John smiled. "There isn't much he doesn't tell me. I'm not only his chief legal officer, we've been friends for years."

Anger bubbled through her numb disbelief. It hurt, knowing Nick had shared the details of their unlikely romance with a business associate. It hurt worse—much worse—hearing about this letter and knowing that all along, Nick had thought Lincoln was mad for considering Deidre his daughter and heir.

She wasn't going to sit here and listen to John while he toyed with her emotions like a cat playing with a mouse before it pounced. She stood abruptly.

"I think you'd better go."

John looked taken aback. He stood slowly. "Of course, if you wish. I didn't mean to insult you in any way—"

"Yes, you did," Deidre replied. Her voice sounded cool and steely to her own ears, but on the inside, she was wilting. She just wanted John Kellerman out of the house so she could try and untangle her chaotic thoughts and emotions about Nick and the letter. Could Nick really have kept such a thing from her? He'd admitted that he possessed a letter from Lincoln and had definitely refused to let her see it—

Her cell phone started to ring. She didn't really think about it, just walked over to the kitchen counter and picked it up instinctively.

"Hello," she said distractedly.

"Ms. Kavanaugh?" a woman on the other end said. "Deidre Kavanaugh?"

"Yes."

"My name is Evelyn Mendez, from GenLabs. We spoke several weeks back?"

Deidre froze. She glanced at John Kellerman. She didn't know precisely what he'd seen on her face, but he'd gone suddenly still and alert.

"Yes, I remember," Deidre managed to get out through numb lips.

"I'm calling with the results of the paternity test, Ms. Kavanaugh."

Time seemed to stretch.

A knock resounded in the silent kitchen. When she just stared at the door blankly, John started and opened it himself.

"What's going on?" Nick asked, glancing from John to Deidre and back to John again.

"Deidre?" Nick repeated when neither John nor she answered his question. Deidre just stood there clutching the phone to her ear. Her face was pale as chalk. What the hell had John been saying to her? He walked toward her, recalling all too well what had happened the last time he'd seen her that pale. Much to his confusion, instead of accepting his support, she backed away from him several steps, her gaze narrowed like she couldn't quite bring him into focus.

"Ms. Mendez, can you hold on for just a moment?" Deidre spoke in a strained tone into the phone, her large eyes trained on Nick. Then, much to Nick's growing concern, she stepped past him, opened the oven and removed a pan of cookies.

"You two will have to excuse me," she said briskly over her shoulder before she left the kitchen. A few seconds later, Nick heard the door to the bedroom close down the hall. He spun around to face John, his mouth open in amazement.

"What the hell did you say to her?" he accused.

"It wasn't me that got her upset," John defended. "It was that phone call. Every bit of color washed out of her face when she got it."

Something flickered in John's blue eyes. An alarm started going off in Nick's head.

"You don't suppose…" John began before he faded off, his alert gaze now trained on the hallway. Nick *did* suppose, and that's what had him worried.

"Didn't I tell you back in San Francisco to mind your own business when it came to Deidre?" Nick asked.

John straightened his tie in a nervous gesture. "DuBois Enterprises *is* my business. It used to be your sole focus as well, Nick."

"Get out of here," Nick growled through clenched teeth. He was mad enough to bite through steel. John must have noticed, because he blanched.

"If you have the right to wait and find out if that's the phone call we've been waiting for, then I certainly—"

"Have no right whatsoever," Nick finished. He stalked over to the coat tree and grabbed John's coat. John started back when he shoved it in the vicinity of his chest. "You're an employee of DuBois Enterprises, and even that's an uncertainty at the moment."

"Are you threatening to fire me?" John asked furiously. "I have a contract!"

"Contracts can be broken. Besides, I doubt I'm the only one you've insulted by coming here. Are you so shortsighted—so dense—to alienate Deidre, when she's your new employer?"

"You don't know that she's my new employer for sure. You don't know that I insulted her," John hissed as he put on his coat. "Maybe it's *you* that she was insulted by."

"What's that supposed to mean?" Nick demanded, narrowing the distance between them in a split second, but he was talking to the older man's back. Apparently, John was remembering all too clearly what Nick had graphically told him he'd do to him if he continued with his subtle threats and innuendos in regard to Deidre.

He slammed the door after the fleeing man, stifling a nearly overwhelming aggressive urge to go after him. He didn't want to leave Deidre.

He couldn't *believe* John had come to Harbor Town to confront her without Nick's knowledge or approval.

He left the kitchen, meeting Deidre as she entered the living room. She came to a halt when she saw him.

"I heard the door slam. Did John leave?" she asked.

His nerves seemed to prickle beneath his skin when he noticed the tightness of her mouth when she spoke, the unusual pallor of her face, the way her usually soulful eyes were shuttered.

"He's gone," Nick said, stepping toward her. She didn't back away from him this time, but he sensed her wariness. "What is it? What's happened? What did John say to you? Deidre?" he prodded when she didn't immediately reply. He didn't care for the way she was detailing his features as if she were seeing him for the first time.

"He told me about the letter."

Her whisper in the silent room struck him like a slashing razor.

"He told me that you believe Lincoln was demented when he made me his heir. He told me that you suspected he was of unsound mind…that the Lincoln you knew would *never* have done such a foolhardy thing as change his will because of a crazy wish that I was his daughter. Is that true?" she asked softly.

"No. I mean…yes, it is partly true." He made a sound of frustration when he saw her shocked expression. "You haven't seen the letter, Deidre."

"Because you wouldn't let me," she said, her subdued voice now vibrating with anger. "I asked to see it. I *wanted* to see it."

"I know," he said in a pressured tone. "But I thought it might upset you."

"So you did it all for my benefit. Is that right, Nick?" she asked, taking a step toward him, her rigid stance portraying her emotional distress.

"Not in the beginning, no," he admitted.

"That letter is apparently crucial potential evidence in a court of law—evidence that Lincoln was of unsound mind when he changed his will. Do you deny it?"

"It is…potentially."

"*That's* why you didn't want me to see it."

Nick clenched his eyes shut, feeling the situation spinning out of control. Damn John Kellerman's conniving interference. He opened his eyes and held Deidre's stare, trying to will her to understand.

"That may have been true in the beginning, when I first came here."

Something flashed in her eyes that looked like hope. "So you *don't* believe Lincoln was of unsound mind? You've changed your opinion?"

Regret spiked through him. "I meant I don't plan to contest the will anymore."

Her crestfallen expression told him she'd noticed he'd

sidestepped her question. The silence that followed weighed on him.

"You mean you don't plan to contest the will, but you still think that Lincoln wasn't of sound mind when he named me his heir and co-owner of DuBois Enterprises—when he claimed me as his daughter?"

The tremor in her voice made every muscle in his body clench tight. He approached her, grasping her shoulders.

"Listen to me," he said with quiet intensity. "I've told you how much Lincoln wanted a family. Am I surprised that he latched on to you as his daughter—the child of the one woman he'd always loved, Brigit Kavanaugh? A beautiful, smart, vibrant woman? *No.* That makes perfect sense to me."

"But you still think he was demented for believing I was his daughter and leaving me half his company?"

He clamped his eyes shut and then opened them, having trouble meeting her gaze. "When I first read that letter? Yes. Maybe I still do a little, to be honest. You haven't seen the letter—it's barely intelligible, disorganized…touching, but in a completely unrealistic, childlike way."

"Unrealistic?" Deidre repeated flatly.

"I thought he was letting wishful thinking rule him instead of rationality. He had no proof you were his daughter but your story. You have no business experience. What's more, you'd told him point-blank you didn't want to run Du-Bois Enterprises," he said, desperate to make her understand.

"That was very convenient for you, wasn't it?" she asked. Through her narrowed lids, Nick saw the glassiness of her eyes. "I said I know nothing about business and am literally blown away by the news that I'm Lincoln's coheir, and you establish that without a doubt, I shouldn't have been given controlling interest in Lincoln's company because I said a few times—as a consequence of shock and sheer ignorance—that I didn't want the job."

"Your saying you didn't want the responsibility wasn't the only thing I was thinking about," Nick rasped. "Lincoln knew you had no business experience whatsoever. He also didn't know you were his daughter. But that's not the point."

Her eyes flashed in anger. "What is the point then, Nick? You seem so clear on the whole matter. Please, grant me some of your infinite wisdom," she bit out sarcastically. "Why can't you just admit that you planned to contest the will all along?"

"Because it's not true! That's not how I viewed things, Deidre. I was ruling things out as I went along. I only planned to make decisions once I had crucial information. I needed to know if you truly were Lincoln's daughter, I needed to be sure of the fact that you hadn't coerced him in any way—"

"And if you established that both of those things were true, you could always fall back on the allegation that Lincoln wasn't of sound mind," Deidre shouted, startling him. She twisted out of his hold and walked toward the fireplace, abruptly turning to face him. His heart seized in his chest. Her expression was shattered. "You never wanted Lincoln to accept me as his daughter. You *never* did," she cried out.

"That's not true—"

"It is true," she said, sounding slightly hysterical. "What must have gone through your mind when I showed up at The Pines, saying I was Lincoln's natural daughter? All those years you spent proving yourself to Lincoln and everyone in his company, all those years being everything to Lincoln. And you *were* everything…everything *but*…" she bit out emphatically, her eyes a little wild.

He knew she was fighting instinctively, like a wounded animal, but anger pierced through his anxiety that she'd chosen that particular insult to throw in his face.

Another glance at her and his fury was gone. Tears were rushing down her cheeks now, but Nick felt helpless to stop or comfort her. Her hurt and confusion seemed too thick to breach.

"Everything *but* Lincoln's natural child," Deidre finished in a hoarse whisper. She tilted her chin up defiantly, but her eyes were wells of pain. "You considered Lincoln to be demented for believing I was his daughter…a wishful old fool."

"Listen to me," he spoke quietly, trying desperately to penetrate her distress. "You didn't read the letter. It was odd… disjointed. He insinuated in it that you and I could have the future that Brigit and he never had."

Dread filled him when her expression turned incredulous. "Deidre, wait—"

"That was your *proof* that he was a madman? That you and I might find something together?" she asked, wide-eyed with shock.

"No! That's not what I meant at all." He cursed under his breath in profound frustration.

"You *did* think it!" she accused.

"What if I did, in the beginning?" he boomed, frustration overwhelming him. "You probably would have thought something similar if you read that letter soon after he'd died. It doesn't matter what I thought then. I'm not going to contest the will. I don't give a *damn* whose daughter you are or aren't. Deidre? Are you listening to me?" he asked when she continued to stare at him like he was invisible.

"Lincoln wasn't a fool," she said as if he hadn't spoken. She wiped her cheek with the back of her hand. Her chin fell to her chest and she took a long inhale. "*I* may have been one for getting involved with you in these…absurd circumstances, but Lincoln wasn't a fool," she repeated under her breath. Her shoulders slumped as if in sudden fatigue.

"Deidre?" he prompted, concern swamping him. "I've told you from the beginning that what's between us is separate from the legalities of Lincoln's will."

She looked up slowly, the anguished defiance he saw in her eyes cutting him to the quick. "How can you stand there and say that to me with a straight face?"

"Because it's true. Lincoln has nothing to do with how we feel about each other. DuBois Enterprises doesn't have anything to do with how we feel about each other. *Deidre?*" he prompted sharply. He had the strangest feeling he was talking to her across an enormous, mile-deep canyon and that she was only hearing the echo of every third word he spoke.

"That call earlier was from GenLabs," she said quietly. "Lincoln was right. I am his biological daughter. I'll make sure you get a copy of the formal report."

Nick watched, frozen to the spot, as she walked past him toward the hallway. A moment later, he heard the latch on her bedroom door shut with a click of finality.

Chapter Eleven

Deidre arrived in Chicago early the next afternoon. It was a gray, blustery winter day that perfectly matched her mood. Marc and Mari lived in a brownstone on a quiet, residential street in the Lincoln Park neighborhood. The cheery Christmas lights and festive decorations on the attractive, affluent homes only seemed to amplify Deidre's numb misery.

Mari stood on the sidewalk while Deidre parked in front of the house, a coat draped haphazardly over her shoulders. She took one look at Deidre's face when she got out of the car and rushed to give her a hug.

"Don't say a word," Mari said. She opened the back door of the sedan and withdrew Deidre's suitcase. "Let's get you inside and make you something hot to drink. Marc is at work and Riley went to Gymboree with her nanny, so we'll have an opportunity to talk."

She hustled Deidre into the elegant brownstone and deposited her bag in the guest bedroom. It wasn't long before the two women sat together before the fireplace with hot mugs of tea warming their hands. Deidre was hesitant to get started with her confession, but once she began, the words seemed to roll out of her of their own volition. Mari listened, her expression becoming increasingly concerned and sober as time passed.

"...I was so confused after Nick left last night that I couldn't think. Thank God I was able to sleep a couple hours. When I woke up today, I only wanted to do one thing—escape," Deidre told Mari in conclusion. "And...well, here I am."

Mari patted her knee, her expression tight with compassion and worry. "You did the right thing, coming here. You know we're always ecstatic to have you. I just wish the circumstances could be different," she said, slumping back in her chair. She glanced at Deidre and shook her head. "I don't know how *anyone* can be expected to balance so many stressful situations in such a short period of time."

"I bet I know what you're thinking," Deidre murmured. "That I was the one who made things worse for myself by getting involved with Nick."

"I wasn't thinking that. I know firsthand that the heart can lead you into some very sticky situations, indeed—look at Marc's and my romance." Mari's gaze sharpened on her. "How do you feel about Nick, Dee? From what you just said, I'm getting the impression you're intensely attracted to each other."

Deidre smiled sadly. "You want to know if there's more to it than lust, you mean?"

"I guess so," Mari conceded.

Deidre took a sip of her tea, her gaze on the flaming logs in the hearth. "On my part, yes," she whispered after a pause.

"And you're angry at yourself for feeling that way?" Mari prompted.

"Wouldn't you be?" Deidre said, meeting her sister-in-law's stare. "I made a fool of myself. I got involved with a man who planned all along to take me to court, who never believed in my claim to be Lincoln's daughter."

"I thought you said Nick wasn't planning to contest the will."

"He did say that, but should I believe him?" she asked Mari desperately. "John Kellerman implied that was Nick's fallback plan all along—to contest the will based on his belief that Lincoln was of unsound mind at the time it was drawn up. He intended to use that letter as evidence of Lincoln's incapacity. That's why he refused to let me see it."

"It *would* have been very upsetting for you to see."

Deidre did a double take and studied Mari's face. "So you think Nick *was* trying to protect me by keeping the letter from me?"

Mari sighed uncertainly and took a sip of her tea. "I think it's possible. I don't know. There is a terrific amount of money and power at stake."

"Exactly," Deidre muttered. "You begin to see why I doubt myself."

"I don't know Nick well enough to say what he'd do, one way or another. You must not feel you know him well enough, either."

A log popped in the silence that followed. Mari persevered when Deidre didn't respond.

"You wouldn't be here in Chicago while he's still in Harbor Town if you didn't think Nick was being duplicitous," Mari prompted.

"He *was* being duplicitous," Deidre stated with more energy than she felt. "He shouldn't have slept with me, knowing what he knew. If he didn't have faith in Lincoln's judgment and planned to contest the will—even if his plans were tenuous—that was crucial information he should have given me before we got involved."

"Nick changed his mind about contesting the will once he got to know you better," Mari said softly. "That's significant, don't you think? I can't help but wonder…"

"What?" Deidre asked when Mari trailed off.

"Well…if the thing that hurt you the most wasn't that Nick had doubts that you were the rightful heir to DuBois Enterprises. It was that Nick doubted the validity of Lincoln's blind faith that you were his daughter."

Deidre stared unseeingly at the flames. Mari's comment hurt, and she couldn't help but suspect it pained her so much because there was an element of truth to it. Mari must have sensed her discomfort because she patted her knee again warmly.

"We don't have to belabor it right now. It's Christmastime," she said, nodding toward the gorgeous nine-foot Douglas fir decorated with lights and ornaments situated to the right of the fireplace. "I'll be doing a special Christmas Eve concert tomorrow afternoon with the symphony. You and Marc can attend together. Ryan couldn't make it for the concert, but he'll be here late tomorrow afternoon. We'll have our own little family Christmas. It'll be nice."

Deidre tried to muster some enthusiasm into her smile, but it was hard.

What would Nick be doing for Christmas, now that she'd fled Harbor Town? Surely he'd return to The Pines or to San Francisco. She hated the idea of him spending the holiday alone in the Starling Hotel.

She chastised herself when she realized how worked up she was getting as she considered the possibility.

She was in the process of unpacking later when her cell phone rang. She cautiously checked the number but didn't recognize it. For a moment, she wavered about answering it. Nick had called three times since their blowup yesterday, and her mother had left yet another message, imploring her to come to her house for Christmas Eve. She dreaded talking to Nick, but she couldn't stop thinking about him.

Had she been wrong to react as she did? What kind of rotten luck did she possess, to fall in love with a man while billions of dollars were at stake? Could she ever completely trust his motives, now that she knew he'd kept his thoughts about Lincoln's letter secret from her?

She felt uncertain about talking to her mother, as well. They'd gotten along so well at the McGraw Stables. What's more, Liam and Natalie would be home for Christmas following their honeymoon. Colleen, Eric and the kids would go to Sycamore Avenue. If things hadn't derailed so drastically yesterday after John's visit and the call from GenLabs, Deidre suspected she'd have been accepting her mom's invitation.

She made a split-second decision and answered the phone. "Hello?"

"Ms. Kavanaugh? Deidre?" Something about the slight quaver in his voice suggested she spoke to an older man.

"Yes?"

"Hello. My name is Abel Warren. I was Lincoln DuBois's personal attorney and am the designated attorney for his estate."

"Oh…hello, Mr. Warren."

"I'm very sorry about your loss, Ms. Kavanaugh."

"Thank you. You knew Lincoln for a very long time, I'm sure. I'm sorry for your loss, as well."

"Lincoln was a good friend. I hope you don't mind me reaching you at this number. Nick Malone gave it to me."

"He did?"

"Yes. He asked me to contact you in regard to several things, one crucial item being the availability of your funds."

"Funds?"

"Yes. Your bank accounts and assets? I previously understood from Nick that we were waiting to hear about paternity testing. However, seeing as how paternity has been confirmed and Nick has given the go-ahead, we are free to carry on."

"But I haven't given you and Nick the official report yet," she said numbly. "GenLabs is sending it special delivery later this afternoon."

"Nick is satisfied with a verbal affirmation, and I'm satisfied if he is. Ms. Kavanaugh?" the man asked when she was too stunned to reply for several seconds. Deidre was too busy absorbing the news that Nick had told the lawyer that her word was golden. Of course she shouldn't be surprised, should she? Nick had insinuated he wouldn't stop her from getting access to Lincoln's inheritance even before the results from the genetic testing had come.

"Yes?"

"I understand from Nick that discovering you are Lincoln's coheir has come as quite a shock to you," he said, his voice gentle. "Becoming an extremely wealthy woman overnight must be bewildering. It might be easy to begin to doubt your own instincts. While I would advise extreme caution, I hope you don't give up on trusting yourself."

Something about the unexpected kindness of the attorney affected her deeply. She gave a ragged laugh. "I'll try," she said.

"Give it time. It'll sink in, slowly. I want you to know that I'm your ally, Deidre. Did you know that I worked for your grandfather, George DuBois, before I went to work for Lincoln?"

"No," she said softly.

"Well I did. So you see, you're the third generation of DuBoises that I'll be offering service to. What do you think of that?"

Deidre smiled. She could almost picture a twinkle in the attorney's eye as he spoke. *Third generation of DuBoises.*

"I think it sounds like I'm very lucky," she said.

He chuckled. "That you are. We'll make an appointment to meet as soon as possible, but first things first. I've made arrangements to make your funds available to you immediately. Here's what we're going to do…"

The next morning Deidre sat with Marc, Mari and Riley at their dining room table eating breakfast. Riley wore a pretty red and white velvet dress for Christmas Eve, but Mari had covered her in so many bibs while she ate that the little girl looked like an adorable patchwork quilt.

"There's nothing in the papers yet mentioning you specifically," Marc said, finishing his perusal of the morning edition. "But there's a small blurb in the business section suggesting that changes are afoot at DuBois Enterprises following Lincoln's death. Apparently a big announcement is about to be made."

"Abel Warren told me yesterday that Nick has scheduled a press conference for the day after Christmas," Deidre said. "He'll make an official announcement in Harbor Town about Lincoln's will." She noticed her brother giving Mari a significant glance. "I know what you're probably thinking," Deidre said quietly, taking a sip of her coffee.

"Oh, yeah? What's that?" Marc asked, his mouth quirked into a grin.

"That Nick certainly is acting very cooperatively for someone who was lying and planning to take me to court."

Riley waved a candy-cane-shaped plush toy and shouted in the ensuing silence.

"He's behaving much more civilly than I would have thought when this whole thing started," Marc admitted neutrally.

She'd told her brother last night about her romantic liaison with Nick, although with not as much detail as she'd given Mari. Deidre could almost cut a knife through her brother's concern when she'd admitted to having an affair with Nick Malone. She suspected he was also disappointed in her lapse in judgment, and that's what really pained her.

"Well, I'll need to get into Orchestra Hall soon," Mari said, checking the clock on the wall. "Do you plan on doing anything before the concert, Deidre?"

"I was considering shopping for a dress. I don't have anything to wear to the concert."

"You can always borrow one of my dresses, but I think it's a terrific idea for you to go shopping," Mari told her with a significant glance. "Breaking in those debit cards Mr. Warren had sent to you this morning will start to get you used to the idea that you have practically unlimited funds at your disposal. You've got to get used to being rich at some point," Mari said when Deidre gave her a dry glance.

"I wasn't going to use any of the cards," she said, referring to Abel's temporary solution to giving her access to her funds. "I have my own money."

"Lincoln DuBois's money *is* your money," Marc said so sharply that she glanced at her brother in surprise. He raised his eyebrows in a quiet challenge. "You're his daughter, Deidre. He wanted you to enjoy the benefits of his wealth. From what you told me, he would have wanted that more than anything. I agree with Mari. The sooner you start to get used to the fact that you're wealthy—that you're Lincoln DuBois's daughter—the sooner you'll start to internalize the change in your circumstances. Forgive me for saying so, but it's an insult to Lincoln's wishes for you to continue to deny his gift to you."

Deidre looked away. She suddenly had an overwhelming wish that Nick was there to reassure her with his solemn, gray-eyed gaze.

* * *

Mari had recommended a designer boutique on Oak Street that Deidre couldn't help but feel was way out of her league. Deidre demurred when the salesclerk showed her a stunning crimson, raw silk dress, but then she'd agreed to try it on, and the gown had sold itself. Its neckline showed off her neck, shoulders and a tasteful amount of chest to good effect, and the faux ermine accents around the arm cuff gave it a Yuletide air. She hadn't entirely believed the salesclerk when she'd told her breathlessly that Deidre looked like a Christmas princess, but Deidre couldn't help but *feel* like one as she stared at herself in the dressing-room mirror.

She'd never purchased a dress as expensive as this one. Slowly she pulled out one of the new cards Abel Warren had sent and stared at it for a few seconds.

"No, wait," Deidre said tensely when the salesclerk reached to take the debit card.

Her hand wavered. It seemed wrong somehow, that a debit card should symbolize Lincoln. *You meant more to me than this,* she thought desperately. *I'll never be able to tell you how much more.*

Almost immediately, she imagined Lincoln replying to her in his matter-of-fact tone.

Well, of course I know. You meant more to me than anything money could ever buy. But the money is my legacy to you. Besides, you wouldn't deny me the pleasure of buying my daughter a Christmas dress, would you?

The salesclerk looked at her like she was a tad "off" when Deidre suddenly gave a bark of laughter and smiled. She handed the woman the debit card.

Thank you, she thought to herself fervently, *and Merry Christmas, Lincoln.*

* * *

Marc wolf-whistled when she joined him downstairs that afternoon wearing her new dress.

"Who'd have guessed there was a goddess hiding under your army fatigues," he joked.

Deidre snorted and gave him a playful slap on the arm. "Who'd have guessed there was an ornery big brother under the facade of a Cook County prosecutor and U.S. senator-to-be?"

She was feeling a little more heartened by the time they left Riley with her nanny and got in a cab. Christmas Eve was definitely in the air, she realized as the cabdriver pulled off the inner drive and into the bustling downtown area. Michigan Avenue was packed with last-minute shoppers and tourists. Christmas lights shone on every tree lining the street. The tiny, white lights, not the old-fashioned color ones, Deidre realized.

She tried to ignore the pang of melancholy that went through her when she thought of Nick's and her Christmas tree standing dark and silent in the Cedar Cottage living room.

All during the concert she had to suppress an urge to ask her brother what the right thing to do was in regard to Nick, her mother...her entire future. She didn't really expect Marc to give her a cut-and-dried answer, but she couldn't help but wish for the impossible.

Mari was going to pick up her brother Ryan at the airport following the concert, so Marc and Deidre returned to the townhouse to get things ready for their arrival. Riley was taking a nap, so they relieved the nanny and followed a couple mealtime preparation instructions Mari had given them. Afterward, they concentrated on whipping the house into a festive condition.

"Why don't you just spill it, Dee," Marc said dryly as he built a fire in the living room and Deidre lit all the Christmas lights.

"Spill what?" Deidre asked, turning toward him. She grabbed her cup of hot apple cider off the mantel and sat down in a chair before the fireplace.

"You were practically vibrating during the concert you were thinking so hard. Why don't you just tell me what's on your mind?" Marc said. He gave the flickering logs and kindling one last poke and tossed the fire iron aside before he took a seat next to her.

She bit her bottom lip uncertainly.

"I've never been undecided in my life," she sighed. "The right choice always seemed so clear to me. I knew without a doubt I wanted to practice nursing, even more specifically, emergency and trauma medicine. I knew I wanted to serve in the military in combat, where my skills would be most needed. I knew I was right in keeping my distance from Mom…." She trailed off hesitantly, but Marc didn't interrupt her thought process. "Or at least, I *thought* I was right. I suppose I just wish the right choices were as clear to me now as they have been in the past."

"I got the impression from something Mom said the other day that you and she had been spending some time together. How was that for you?" Marc asked.

"Uncomfortable at first. But it was getting better. Much better," she said softly, watching as the fire spread through the kindling. She sighed. "Sometimes I wish I could just go back to the Middle East or Europe…forget this whole bizarre situation with Lincoln making me an heiress…forget…"

"Nick Malone?"

Deidre glanced at her brother. He looked carelessly handsome sitting there in his shirtsleeves and dress pants. It struck her that he was starting to look very much like Derry Kavanaugh had in his prime—confident and easy with himself, the type of man people instinctively trusted and respected. Her heart seemed to squeeze in her chest at the poignant re-alization of the inevitable passage of time.

"You think I was a fool to ever trust Nick, don't you?"

Marc didn't respond immediately. She could sense him choosing his words in the silence.

"You're wondering if *you* can trust him," Marc said. "I can't be the one to tell you that, Deidre. Only you can know that. I have faith in *you,* if that helps any."

She met his stare and smiled. "Thanks."

"Don't mention it," he said with a small grin.

They sat in companionable silence for a moment.

"Do you think that Mom and Dad trusted each other after their affairs…I mean, *really* trusted?" Deidre asked him.

Marc inhaled slowly. "Mom has told me that she took a vow to forget the past and move ahead with Dad. I believe it was true on both of their parts. I never caught the slightest hint when I was a kid that they weren't completely devoted to each other," Marc said. "Did you?"

Deidre shook her head, staring at the growing flames. "That's what made discovering the truth about Lincoln that much more devastating."

Marc grunted in agreement.

"Poor Dad. I can't imagine how it must have hit him," she whispered.

Marc's head came around.

"You and Dad always had a special bond," Marc said. "The tragedy was, Dad never lived to come to terms with the truth and recognize you would always be his daughter. Always."

"Do you think he would have eventually understood that?" Deidre asked in a hushed tone.

"I have no doubt," Marc said firmly. "Did I ever tell you that Dad and I had a stupid argument before he died? We fought about where I should go to law school. For a few years afterward, I was haunted by the idea that a petty fight was our last interaction. Did he die with anger in his heart toward me? Over time, I've realized the insignificant spats of a minute or a day can't begin to diminish the ocean of love a parent has for a child. Having Riley assured me of that." He met Deidre's gaze. "You were Derry Kavanaugh's daughter. *That* was what was truly in his heart when he died. That, and all his love for you."

Deidre sniffed. Marc smiled and dug in his pocket for a handkerchief. He handed it to her, but when he didn't immediately relinquish it, she looked into his face.

"Lincoln DuBois was a wonderful man, too, from all I've gathered," Marc said. "I imagine if we had the ability to see into his heart, we'd see that you were his daughter, as well. You've experienced a lot of heartache and loss in your life, Dee. I know it hurts, losing both Derry and Lincoln. But in the end, they were *both* your fathers."

A tremor of emotion shuddered through her. Marc was right. She'd always considered herself to be the odd child out, different, fatherless.

But in reality, she'd been blessed with *two* wonderful fathers…and a mother who loved her very much.

Deidre took the handkerchief and patted her damp cheeks. "You know what?" she asked as she stood. "I just made a decision about something."

"What?"

"I'm going back to Harbor Town."

Marc blinked. "To Sycamore Avenue?"

Deidre nodded, drying the tears off her cheeks one last time, and handed back the handkerchief. "Yes, but to the Starling Hotel first. I'm hoping Nick is still there, and that he forgives me for acting so…"

She faded off at the sound of people entering the front

door. A moment later, Mari entered the living room followed by her older brother, Ryan.

"Merry Christmas," Ryan said.

"Merry Christmas!" Deidre went over to greet them, going up on her tiptoes to give Ryan a hug after not seeing him for half a lifetime.

"You and Mari are just alike," Deidre told Ryan warmly when they parted and inspected each other. "I wouldn't have thought she could get more beautiful, just like I wouldn't have thought you could get more handsome. You both had to go and prove me wrong."

"I can't believe it," Ryan said, looking down at her with a teasing glint in his dark eyes. "Is this the same little girl with braces and a perpetual skinned knee who used to rise to every one of Marc's and my dares?"

"Always used to top you guys doing them, too," Deidre shot back, noticing when Marc and Ryan shared a grin. She winked at Mari. Maybe this Christmas would be the one where the two men finally found a new path to friendship.

"Deidre was just telling me she's going back to Harbor Town," Marc said.

"What?" Mari asked, her smile fading.

"I'm so sorry, Mari. Would you mind very much? It's just that..." She waved her hand lamely. "I suddenly realized that Harbor Town is where I should be this Christmas Eve."

"I started thinking, maybe we should head that way, too," Marc said, looking from Ryan to Mari. "The family will be there. It'd be a good opportunity to break our news," he said, giving Mari a significant glance. "What do you two think?"

Mari's mouth opened in amazement. "Well, I'm sure Ryan doesn't want to go to Harbor Town—"

"I'd like to go," Ryan said.

Deidre, Marc and Mari all glanced at Ryan in amazement.

The circumstances of Ryan's last Harbor Town visit, and his encounter with the Kavanaughs, had not been pleasant.

"Are you sure?" Mari murmured.

"Yeah," Ryan said firmly. "There's something important I need to do in the area. I was planning to go back to Michigan on this visit. Might as well be tonight."

Mari's bewildered expression faded as she checked her watch. "Well, we could make it if we hurry, I guess."

Deidre beamed. "I need to go pack and get on the road, then. I'll meet you guys at Mom's? I have to make a quick stop at Cedar Cottage first." She paused to touch her brother's arm. Words wouldn't suffice. She smiled her profound thanks at Marc before she rushed upstairs, her heart racing at the prospect of seeing Nick again.

But would he still be in Harbor Town?

Several hours later, Brigit approached Nick, who stood next to the glowing Kavanaugh Christmas tree. Deidre's mother looked very pretty wearing a dark green dress and an anxious, excited expression.

"She'll be here soon," Brigit assured him, referring to Deidre.

Marc, Mari, Riley and Ryan Itani had arrived on Sycamore Avenue fifteen minutes ago, giving the gathered family a wonderful Christmas surprise. Brigit had been visibly moved by the news that her eldest daughter had decided to join the family for the first time in years.

Nick thought he'd been just as affected by the news, even if he hadn't showed it like Brigit had.

He'd reluctantly agreed to come to Brigit's for Christmas Eve when she'd called, but now he was having serious doubts. He had no reason to believe Deidre would be happy about his unexpected presence at a family gathering.

"I'm worried about those reporters I've been giving the

slip," he said quietly to Brigit "They've gotten wind of the fact that a big story is about to break at DuBois Enterprises. So far they don't seem to be attaching any significance to Deidre, but I wouldn't be surprised at anything at this point," he added under his breath, thinking of John Kellerman. It'd undoubtedly been Kellerman who had leaked the story about Nick being in Harbor Town, trying to put pressure on Nick to make a final decision in regard to the will and possibly to embarrass Nick by putting his and Deidre's relationship in the limelight.

"I'm sure she'll be fine. Marc was just telling me Deidre might arrive a little later than them. She wanted to stop somewhere first, but Marc didn't say—"

Everyone in the crowded living room glanced toward the foyer when they heard the front door opening. Nick instinctively took a step toward the hallway, but forced himself to pause when he recalled that Deidre wouldn't be thrilled at all to see him at a homecoming that was already bound to be emotionally trying for her.

Colleen ducked out of the room to meet her sister. A moment later, Deidre appeared in the opened French doors, her face alight as she gazed at her family members assembled in the large, festively decorated living room.

Her gaze landed on Nick and stuck.

A few seconds stretched. He'd never seen anything so amazing in his life as the sight of Deidre standing there in a regal red dress, all vestiges of the defiant, fierce waif gone, in their place a poised, stunning woman. But no—it wasn't the dress that had made the change. It was the light of hope and forgiveness in her eyes as she stared at him.

Time unstuck. Brigit rushed toward her daughter. Deidre's hug seemed every bit as loving as her mother's. Nick remained standing between the Christmas tree and fireplace, watching as Deidre exclaimed in excitement upon seeing Natalie and Liam—both of them tanned from their honeymoon and grinning from ear to ear—and hugged them enthusiastically. She hugged Brendan and Jenny next, her eyes going wide as though she'd remembered something at the sight of the children. She left the living room and returned a moment later with a large bag filled with Christmas gifts.

"Will you put these under the tree?" she asked the children, smiling.

Brendan gladly relieved her of her burden while Brigit bustled into the kitchen to get Deidre some hot cider. Deidre straightened and smoothed her dress, her gaze immediately finding Nick's. Her sloping shoulders gleamed in the luminescent Christmas lights as she came toward him. He experienced a strong urge to feel the heat from her smooth, flushed cheeks beneath his fingertips.

He couldn't take his eyes off her. Colleen, who had walked up to her sister to talk, glanced over to where Deidre stared at him fixedly and turned away, unnoticed by Deidre.

"Hi," Deidre said, her lips trembling slightly.

"Hi. Merry Christmas," Nick said.

"Merry Christmas."

Her eyes shone like beacons. He opened his mouth to speak, and so did she, but Brigit chose that moment to come toward them with a cup of steaming hot cider.

"I've laid dinner out on the sideboard, buffet-style," Brigit told Deidre.

"Just like when we were kids," Deidre murmured, taking a sip of her cider.

"Come on, you must be starved," Brigit urged, taking her hand.

Nick was heartened to see Deidre hesitate and glance back at him.

"Your mother has already fed me. I'll wait for you here," he said, damning the crowd of people and surrounding festivities, but glad to see Deidre's hand entwined with her mother's.

"Okay," Deidre replied, granting him that small smile that always pierced straight through him to someplace deep.

He inhaled slowly and reminded himself to be patient. This was an important night in Deidre's life, and he couldn't be selfish and whisk her aside to assure himself that was truly forgiveness he saw shining in her lovely eyes.

Even if that's precisely what he wanted to do.

A half an hour later, Deidre stood next to Nick by the Christmas tree. He'd asked her if she'd wanted to sit down when she'd returned from eating, but Deidre had shaken her head. Her heart felt full. She was content just to stand next to Nick, watching her entire family as they chatted and joked and ate cake while Christmas music played in the background. She was happy to see that Ryan Itani seemed comfortable enough, chatting with Eric, Brendan and Colleen. Even Nick and he had spoken for a spell about their common experience as ex–air force pilots.

She stepped closer to the silent, somber man who stood next to her, her shoulder brushing against his upper arm. Her heart hitched when he put his arm around her waist.

They looked at one another, and it was as if they shared a mutual, unspoken message.

Later.

Following Kavanaugh Christmas tradition, Brendan, Jenny and Riley were allowed to open one gift beneath the tree. Much to the children's regret—perhaps Riley's most of all—the rest of the gifts would have to wait until Christmas Day.

"May I have everyone's attention please?" Eric Reyes called once they'd cleaned up the discarded wrapping paper. He walked into the room carrying a bottle of champagne.

Colleen was behind him with a tray of flutes. Brendan and Jenny followed, Jenny holding a plate of what looked like chocolate truffles and Brendan with a towel comically draped over his forearm like a waiter. Colleen and Eric set down their loads.

"The four of us have an announcement we'd like to make," Eric said, putting his arm around Colleen. Jenny giggled in irrepressible excitement. Deidre glanced up at Nick in bewilderment and dawning pleasure.

"Brendan, do you want to start?" Eric asked the twelve-year-old boy.

Brendan nodded, taking a deep breath. "Eric asked Jenny and I for permission for Mom's hand *and* to become our father."

"And we said yes!" Jenny piped up excitedly.

"And then he remembered to ask me about the whole thing, and I said yes, too," Colleen added, looking at Eric with laughter and profound love in her eyes. "So I guess it's official all around. We're going to become a family!"

An uproar ensued. Everyone converged on the couple to offer their congratulations. Nick and Deidre accepted a glass of champagne and joined in a toast. The living room was filled with Christmas music and happy chatter. From the periphery of her vision, Deidre noticed Marc and Mari share a meaningful smile. Mari set her champagne glass on the coffee table.

"Wait…" Deidre said slowly. "Marc and Mari—you two said you had something you wanted to announce here tonight, as well. What is it?"

Mari laughed and shook her head. "It'll wait for another time."

Colleen stared at Mari's discarded champagne flute. "Mari, are you pregnant again?" she blurted out, her blue-green eyes wide.

Ryan leaned forward to look at his sister, his brow creased. "What's this? You're going to have a baby?" he asked.

Laughter escaped Mari's throat as she stared at Colleen and Ryan in amazement.

"Colleen, we didn't want to take the shine off yours and Eric's amazing news—"

"So you *are* pregnant?" Deidre demanded.

Mari glanced from expectant face to expectant face and finally looked at her husband. Marc just shrugged.

"Well...yes," Mari said.

Another uproar ensued. After everyone had gotten over their exclamations and congratulations, they basked in the glow of their good fortune. Brigit put her arm around Deidre, so that she was bracketed by her mother on one side and Nick on the other.

"This has to be the most wonderful Christmas ever. All this wonderful news—and you're *here,* Deidre, hearing it. Maybe that's the most wonderful news of all," Brigit said quietly to Deidre, her heart in her eyes.

Deidre stepped back and located a small, dark red foil package from beneath the tree. She handed it to Brigit.

"What's this?" Brigit asked. "The adults don't open gifts until tomorrow, you know that."

"I have a lot of making up to do in the gift-giving department for a lot of Christmases, so I didn't think it could wait a night longer. Merry Christmas, Mom. It's from Lincoln. And Nick and I."

Nick glanced at her in surprise. Deidre smiled. Tears brimmed in Brigit's blue eyes as she unwrapped the package with trembling fingers. Everyone in the room paused to watch. Brigit gasped when she withdrew the exquisite diamond brooch of the horse in full gallop.

"Oh...it's Lily DuBois's brooch of Gallant Hunter," Brigit cried, tears spilling down her cheek.

Deidre started in surprise. "You recognize it?"

Brigit nodded, her throat convulsing with emotion. "You forget, I grew up with Lincoln. I remember when Gallant Hunter was inducted into the Racing Hall of Fame. I saw Lily wearing this brooch on several occasions. Oh, but you should have it, Deidre. It belonged to your grandmother," Brigit insisted.

Deidre grabbed her mother's wrist when she tried to hand it back to her. She folded Brigit's hand over the brooch. "No. I want you to have it. Lincoln would have wanted that. I just know it."

"I agree completely," Nick said.

Deidre took the brooch and pinned it to her mother's dress, where it sparkled brilliantly next to the dark green fabric. "There. Perfect."

Brigit hugged her with feeling. Deidre closed her eyes and inhaled the familiar scent of her mother's perfume. She'd wondered and worried what the wise choice was in regard to her mother. Because of the feeling that swelled in her at that moment, Deidre knew without a doubt that forgiveness had been the supremely right thing.

When mother and daughter broke from their hug, Deidre kept her arm around Brigit's waist and put the other around Nick. He leaned down and spoke into her ear, his deep, gruff voice causing a shiver of pleasure to go through her.

"You're something else, do you know that?"

She looked up at him and met his stare. "I was so glad to see you when I walked in," she whispered. "You never did tell me how you ended up here tonight."

Nick nodded in the direction of her mother and spoke very quietly. "Brigit and I ran into each other getting coffee at Celino's this morning. When she heard you'd left town, I think she took pity on me. Maybe she thought we could suffer together instead of apart, knowing you'd likely be gone on Christmas Eve."

Deidre took in his features, cherishing every one. Then she swept her gaze across her family.

She saw Liam nuzzle Natalie's cheek until she turned to face him. "Merry Christmas, wife," Deidre heard him murmur before he kissed Natalie.

Marc took the opportunity of the lull in the conversation to kiss Mari with feeling. At the same moment, Eric dipped his head down to his new fiancée's upturned face.

"There's mistletoe back there on the chandelier," Brigit said confidentially to Deidre and Nick, nodding a few feet behind them. "It seems to have very good effect, even from a distance." Brigit gave them a droll smile and left the room.

Deidre was left looking up at Nick.

"Merry Christmas," she whispered before she went up on her toes and touched her mouth to his, praying he understood the volumes of unspoken words that accompanied her kiss.

Epilogue

When they left that night, Nick convinced Deidre to leave her car at her mother's since they'd return there the following morning for Christmas Day. The tension between them mounted as they drove through a picturesque Harbor Town. The little community might have been placed under a spell. It was silent and seemed to sparkle with Christmas magic.

Of course that special gleam that gilded the entire world might have been projected by Deidre herself, she felt so happy.

"Aren't we going to Cedar Cottage?" Deidre asked when Nick turned onto Main Street instead of continuing on Travertine Drive.

"No. I thought we'd go to the hotel, if you don't mind. There's something there I need to get. The only problem is," he said as he turned into the Starling Hotel parking lot, "you might have to join me in a little cloak-and-dagger routine to avoid the reporters that have been gathering here. They keep thinking I'll spill the truth about the will if they pounce on me hard enough. We'll take the stairs up to my suite."

While they were hurrying down the hallway a minute later, Nick spied a reporter standing in the lobby in the distance, talking on his cell phone. He rapidly put his back to the wall and Deidre followed his example. She stifled some giggles as they cautiously made their way to the doorway leading to the back stairs.

"Shhh," Nick hushed, but he was grinning, too.

They ducked into Nick's suite on the fifth floor, both of them breathless with laughter and the exertion of climbing the stairs. Deidre gazed around the large, luxurious suite and found the bathroom door.

"I'm just going to pop in here and freshen up a little," she said, laughter still lingering around her mouth.

When she came out a few minutes later, Nick was standing behind the granite wet bar.

"Champagne?" she asked, her eyes going wide.

"Yeah. I thought it was appropriate," Nick told her, a small smile shaping his mouth. His longish bangs had fallen on his forehead as he uncorked the bottle. He really was the most handsome man she'd ever seen. How she could have ever considered him cold and heartless was beyond her.

She smiled as he came around the bar and handed her a flute of champagne.

"Did you mean champagne was appropriate because it's Christmas Eve?" she asked.

He shook his head, holding her stare. He waved her over to a seating area where they both sat on a plush couch.

"What's the appropriate occasion then?" Deidre asked.

Nick shrugged and her gaze dropped over his broad shoulders. He looked good enough to eat wearing a well-cut black suit, crisp white dress shirt and a silver-gray tie that almost matched the color of his eyes.

"For a couple of things, I guess."

"Such as?" Deidre prompted.

"First, to say I'm sorry."

"I'm sorry, too, Nick."

"I was too amazed and pissed off about the idea of John Kellerman coming here to sabotage everything, I couldn't even think straight. I missed the opportunity to set things right with you the other night."

"I couldn't think either," she said. She studied the bubbling fluid in the flute, too ashamed to meet his eyes. "I was too busy panicking. I was more than mad. I was scared. I was scared of what it meant if *you*—the person who was closest to Lincoln—doubted the soundness of his mind when he'd convinced himself I was his daughter."

"Sometimes the people who are closest have the most trouble seeing the truth about the other," he murmured.

"I was afraid of other things," she said quietly. "I was scared you'd been keeping secrets from me…manipulating me."

He put his arm around her and stroked the skin on her shoulder just next to her dress. She suppressed a shiver of pleasure at his touch.

"I thought I told you never to be scared when it comes to me," he said.

She gave a small smile. "I guess it temporarily slipped my mind. Once I got to Chicago and I started to see things more clearly, I realized you were hardly acting like a person who was using me. Just the opposite, in fact."

He laughed, low and rough. "If I had been smart, I would have known there was one thing I could have told you that day at Cedar Cottage that would have reassured you that I wasn't plotting against you."

"What's that?"

"That I've fallen in love with you."

Deidre froze.

"You…you have?"

"I think I'm concussed I fell so hard," he said dryly under his breath.

He sounded so starkly earnest, Deidre couldn't help but smile.

"So the thing of it is, it would be pretty stupid of me to take you to court or hassle you or do anything that wasn't in the service of your complete happiness, wouldn't it?" he murmured. Her breath stuck in her lungs when he leaned forward and kissed her with warm, firm lips. "I only want you to be happy, Deidre. Please believe me."

"I do," she whispered.

"I know the fact that we're Lincoln's coheirs has muddied up the waters. I know people like Nick Kellerman are going to raise their eyebrows and hiss about our relationship. But I don't care. Lincoln was wise to split things between us fifty-fifty."

"I still don't want to run DuBois Enterprises, Nick. That's your job. Lincoln knew no one could do it better than you. He trusted you, and so do I."

"You still have half of the controlling interest. That's never going to change. If you ever decide to take the helm with me at DuBois, I'll be more than happy to share. You can change your mind whenever you like—our marriage won't change that."

She smiled and kissed him again fervently.

"There's something else," Nick said quietly next to her lips. He withdrew his arm from around her and took her champagne glass, setting it on the table beside him and leaning back on the couch. Deidre met his stare.

"I know being Lincoln's daughter meant the world to you," Nick said. "But the fact of the matter is, I don't care whose daughter you are. I just want you to be my wife. Marry me, Deidre."

She felt him place something in her hand. She stared in numb disbelief at the signature light blue Tiffany jewelry box. Her hand shook as she opened it. Teardrops skittered down her cheek when she saw the stunning pavé ring with the sparkling large diamond set in the middle.

She looked at Nick and saw the question lingering in his eyes.

"Yes," she whispered emphatically.

His mouth tilted in a smile. He reached for the box and removed the ring.

"It fits perfectly," she said when he slid it on her finger a moment later.

"I got lucky. I bought it in San Francisco while I was there. I've been carrying it around, waiting for the best time to give it to you."

"You have?" Deidre asked in amazement. She thought of his intense lovemaking when he'd returned home early from San Francisco. He'd known…even then.

"I kicked myself numb after what happened with John Kellerman for not giving it to you sooner. Then everything went to hell, and you left town, and I wondered if I'd lost the chance."

"But you didn't. I love you, Nick," she said feelingly before she threw her arms around his neck and kissed him. A moment later, they separated, both of them slightly breathless. Nick grinned at her unabashedly.

"Are you sure you want to do this?" she asked, laughing because so much happiness was inside her that it was brimming over. "Won't everyone at DuBois think it's foolish of us to mix business and romance?"

"Maybe," he said shrugging. "People will hear the news of our engagement and assume you turned my head. Once they catch a glimpse of you, they'll know why, and shut up after a spell."

Deidre gave him a repressive glance.

"It's true. I told you before—I'm a man, not a job. But there's no reason whatsoever our getting married has to affect the running or prosperity of DuBois Enterprises. Lincoln always kept DuBois a private business. It was his dream to make it a family-run one. Now his dream will come true. I've never been surer of anything in my life," he said quietly. "You?"

"I feel the same way," she said in a whisper, every trace of her doubt vanished.

Nick picked up their champagne glasses and handed one to her.

"Let's make a toast. To Lincoln."

"To Lincoln," she murmured. She tapped her flute to his and they both drank.

"I'm beginning to realize you were right about Linc. At first, I thought he was mad for mentioning you and me in that letter—for suggesting that two people who were virtual strangers might share the happiness that wasn't meant to be between your mother and him."

"And now?" Deidre asked quietly as he removed her flute from her hand and set it back on the table. He took her into his arms and kissed her damp cheeks. Deidre lifted her head and their mouths brushed together.

"Now I think he might have been the wisest man on the face of the earth for throwing us together."

Her blissful laughter was cut off beneath Nick's all-consuming kiss.

* * * * *

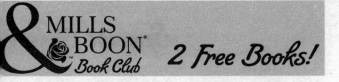

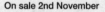

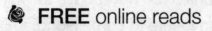

The World of Mills & Boon®

There's a Mills & Boon® series that's perfect for you. We publish ten series and, with new titles every month, you never have to wait long for your favourite to come along.

Blaze.
Scorching hot, sexy reads
4 new stories every month

By Request
Relive the romance with the best of the best
9 new stories every month

Cherish™
Romance to melt the heart every time
12 new stories every month

Desire™
Passionate and dramatic love stories
8 new stories every month

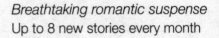